For more than forty years,
Yearling has been the leading name
in classic and award-winning literature
for young readers.

Yearling books feature children's
favorite authors and characters,
providing dynamic stories of adventure,
humor, history, mystery, and fantasy.

Trust Yearling paperbacks to entertain,
inspire, and promote the love of reading
in all children.

LITTLE FUR

The Legend Begins

ISOBELLE CARMODY

A YEARLING BOOK

Visit us on the Web! www.randomhouse.com/kids

Educators and librarians, for a variety of teaching tools, visit us at
www.randomhouse.com/teachers

ISBN: 978-0-375-83855-2

Reprinted by arrangement with Random House Books for Young Readers

Printed in the United States of America

January 2008

10 9 8 7 6 5 4 3 2 1

First Yearling Edition

For Adelaide, my own little elf girl . . .

CONTENTS

CHAPTER 1
The Secrets of Trees

In the middle of a great, sprawling gray city was a place that no human had ever entered.

It looked like a trackless wilderness humped up at the center and edged in tangled bushes knitted together by a winding creeper. Sometimes people talked of getting rid of the wilderness, but it was almost impossible for humans to think about it long enough to act. The only way they managed it was if two or more of them thought it together. But as soon as they went away from one another, it slipped from their minds.

The power that protected the wilderness came from seven ancient trees. They were all that remained of a marvelous grove of singing trees, which had once been part of a forest that had covered the land. Then humans came and cut down trees to make room for their black roads and high houses. The forest shrank, but the earth magic that had flowed through the dead trees did not vanish. It was absorbed by the trees that remained until the seven singing trees were so saturated in magic that they were able to sink their roots deep enough into the ground to touch the earth spirit. When the earth spirit heard the song of the trees' sorrow, it bestowed upon them the power to dim the idea of the wilderness in the minds of humans, and so the chopping ended.

In time, the small wilderness became home to hundreds of creatures.

One was an elf troll called Little Fur. As tall as a three-year-old human child, she had slanted green eyes, wild red hair that brambled about

her pointed ears and bare, broad, four-toed feet.

Little Fur loved the seven ancient trees, and tended them carefully. She poured cool water over their exposed roots on hot, dry days, and when snow blanketed the wilderness in winter, she sang to them of summer days to come. The trees did not need her protection, but they loved her as only trees can love. They themselves sang no more, but when she rested her cheek upon their gnarled bark, they whispered to her of the world that lay beyond the wilderness.

Little Fur was a healer. Within the wilderness she brought water and seeds to bare patches of earth and looked after new plants by pulling the grass aside to give them breathing space. She collected herbs to make poultices, salves and tisanes, and as she treated the wounds of small animals and birds that came seeking her help, she would sing to them, knowing that a wound to the body was only part of what was hurt. The spirit also needed healing.

Most of the creatures who came to her from outside the wilderness blamed their hurts on humans or upon their devices and machines, so that Little Fur sometimes wondered if the damaging of small things was their sole purpose and delight. It troubled her very much that one of her best friends, a shaggy pony called Brownie, belonged to a human and spoke kindly of it. But it was the same with many of the beasts and birds who had been born as the slaves and companions of humans.

Brownie's human had brought him and his brothers from a city by the sea to live in a park where they gave rides to small humans. He pulled them to and fro in a cart, but the other two ponies, being bigger, wore saddles and carried older children on their backs.

The pony field almost touched fingertips with the westernmost point of the park, and it was the smell of wildness that lured Brownie to jump his low fence one night and gallop over the black road to see what had caused it.

Little Fur was sitting quietly on one of the small hill meadows, waiting for the exact moment some yellow evening primroses opened, when Brownie came thundering down the moonlit slope, kicking his heels up and neighing and tossing his mane until steam rose like mist from his hot coat. Only when he stopped to tear at a mouthful of grass did he catch the scent of Little Fur. She did not smell of badness, but his nose told him that she was some sort of troll and he had always thought the smell of badness *was* the smell of troll.

"What are you?" Brownie asked warily.

"I am an elf troll," Little Fur said, smelling on him the same salty, sour odor that came from the cats and birds who lived with humans.

"I have never heard of an elf troll," Brownie said.

"My father was an elf," Little Fur explained.

"An elf!" exclaimed Brownie. "A sea sprite told me they built boats shaped like swans and sailed away when humans came."

"What is a sea sprite?" Little Fur asked.

"One of those things left over from the age

before humans came. Like you and mermaids and pixies. There are not many of you left. I wish I could meet your father."

"He and my mother went away when I was very small," Little Fur said.

"I suppose he went over the sea with the other elves," said Brownie. "But your mother could not have gone if she was a troll."

"What about you?" Little Fur interrupted. The pony's talk about her parents made her feel strange. "Did you escape from the humans?"

Brownie told her about jumping over the barrier that held him and his brothers, and then he said, "I will go back before morning so that my human does not make it too high to jump. That way I will be able to come again."

"Why don't you stay, now that you have escaped?" Little Fur asked, astonished that he would talk of *going back* just like the cats and birds who had lived with humans.

"I like my human and I could not leave my two brothers," Brownie said.

Little Fur did not know what to say. The idea of being owned by a human seemed dreadful to her. Her greatest fear was that humans would someday enter the wilderness and lay it to waste.

Brownie came a step nearer and asked, "You are not bad, then?"

"Can't you smell the answer?" Little Fur asked him with pity, knowing that creatures who dwelt with humans lost their proper sense of smell, so that they could only smell *things*, and not thoughts and ideas and feelings.

"You don't smell like the bad trolls that used to live in the city by the sea," Brownie said. "But there are many more trolls here and they might have learned to hide the smell of their badness."

"There are thousands of trolls here," Little Fur said. "They hide in drains and sewers and cellars in a network of tunnels beneath the city. And deeper down are great caverns unknown to humans, where the trolls have made a city of their own. Yet they cannot hide the smell of their badness. I don't think that's possible."

"Aren't you afraid to live where there are so many trolls?" Brownie asked, glancing around as if a storm of trolls might come boiling out of the night shadows.

Little Fur laughed. "Trolls never come here. They hate green and growing things almost as much as they hate the sunlight."

"I wonder what they did before there were human cities to hide in," Brownie murmured.

"Trolls were here before the earth spirit woke," Little Fur said. "When green things began to grow, they hated it. They burrowed deep into places where the earth magic could not reach them, but the ground was wrong and it hurt them and made them sick. They were almost extinct when humans started making cities."

"How do you know about such things?" Brownie asked.

Little Fur led Brownie deeper into the wilderness, which was larger than it looked from the outside, for the land within it was folded like a blanket. They climbed the mounded hill at its center and Brownie saw that there was a deep hollow inside it. At its base grew a dense grove of trees.

It was not until he had followed Little Fur down a rabbit track winding into the hidden hollow that he discovered there were only seven great trees growing there. The trunk of a single one was bigger than the stable where he slept with his brothers, and the enormous branches sprouting from the trunks were themselves as big as trees. Each branch forked into smaller and smaller branches, all of them heavy with leaves. Each tree wove and braided its branches together with those of neighboring trees to form a dense canopy. When one was standing under it, nothing could be seen of the sky, and the light was as green and heavy as syrup. It made Brownie feel that he wanted to stand still and put down roots, too.

He rested his muzzle against the velvety green moss pelt of one of the trees, as Little Fur urged, and was stunned to hear the tree whispering, though he could not make out its words.

"You have to make your mind quiet and sort of let it float into the tree," she explained, but Brownie was too impatient with excitement to try. He said it was enough for him to know that such trees existed.

Brownie came often to the wilderness after that, and he and Little Fur talked of the world beyond it. Brownie was very proud of his worldliness. By worldliness, Little Fur came to understand, he meant wisdom, though she was not always sure that knowing a lot about the world was the same as being wise.

They spoke of humans more than any other subject. Or perhaps it is more fair to say that Little Fur interrogated Brownie on the subject of humans. Sometimes she had nightmares after their talks, but it was better to learn as much as she could, in the hope of being able to protect herself and her beloved wilderness from them.

Brownie scoffed at her fears, saying humans were not bad, but whether they were or were not, nothing he said ever made her think of them as anything but dangerous.

CHAPTER 2

Smoke!

Brownie always wanted to talk about Little Fur's father, for he was enchanted by the idea that she was part elf. He liked to make up stories of how her parents had fallen in love and what terrible fate had befallen them to orphan her. In time his stories ceased to discomfit her, and she even came to enjoy them.

For her part, Little Fur loved hearing Brownie talk of the sea. He spoke very poetically of waves and wind. He claimed that the wilderness reminded him of the ocean. This was something

Little Fur never quite understood, for how could a great, restless body of water such as he described be like the wilderness that was her home?

"I will take you on my back to a place where you can smell the waves," Brownie announced one day.

"It is impossible," Little Fur answered.

"It is too far to go to the sea," Brownie agreed. "But I can carry you to a stream that goes to the sea, and you will smell the waves in it."

"I can't ride on your back," Little Fur said.

Brownie protested that he would never let her fall.

"It's not that, but if I climbed onto your back, I would lose touch with the flow of earth magic."

"It would only be for a little time," Brownie said.

"A moment would be too long, for the earth magic would never flow through me again," Little Fur said.

Brownie gaped at her. "Do you mean that you

have to be touching the ground *all the time*?"

"My skin has always been in touch with brown earth where things can grow, or with green or growing things," she said.

"Always?"

"Always," Little Fur said.

"How do you know you wouldn't be able to get back in touch with the flow if you went away from it, then? After all, I feel it now, and yet I go away from it when I go into my stable, or when I walk on the black roads."

"I am part troll," Little Fur said.

Brownie asked in a low voice, "What would happen if you . . . did lose touch with the flow of earth magic?"

"I should have to leave the wilderness. The Old Ones will abide nothing here that cannot accept the flow of earth magic," Little Fur said.

Brownie was appalled. "But . . . Little Fur, what if you forget yourself and jump up in the air?"

"Why would I want to?" Little Fur responded simply.

16

"For joy!" Brownie cried, and pranced and reared and capered to show her what she was missing out on. But Little Fur only laughed and clapped her hands, saying that it made her heart leap and gallop to see *him* prancing and jumping, just as it made her heart fly to see Crow take to his wings.

Crow was Little Fur's other great friend. She had found him at the foot of a tree after a storm, and nursed him until he stopped seeing three of everything. Crow was loud, boastful, conceited and opinionated. Yet, like Brownie, he was occupied, if somewhat giddily, with more than food and mates. He, too, dwelt among humans, but he regarded the city as a roost for birds, and saw humans as stupid, dangerously clumsy creatures who were of no consequence except as a source of bread crusts and scraps. But because of Little Fur's interest in humans, Crow had taken to describing their activities to her.

And so it was Crow who brought the first news of the tree burners.

"A pack of humans burning trees?" Little Fur echoed, refusing to react too much. Crow liked to present news in the most dramatic way in order to make sure everyone was listening to him.

"Craaak! They creeping out at night and burning trees up!" Crow screamed.

Beginning to be alarmed, Little Fur questioned the bird closely and learned that he had gotten his information from a possum who lived in the roof of an old human. She had heard the news from the human's talking picture box, which was very loud. Never exactly sure what a picture box was, Little Fur had learned enough to know that this was one of the ways humans communicated news.

"Are you sure the possum heard it right?" she asked. Humans' speech was very difficult to understand, even for those animals who lived with them.

"Maybe not," Crow said unhelpfully. "Possums being almost as stupid as humans."

"Did the talking picture box say why the human pack burns trees?" Little Fur asked.

Crow rolled his eyes. "They *liking* to burn! That being reason enough for humans. But Old Ones not letting tree killers coming here."

Little Fur shook her head. "A pack of humans all thinking about finding trees to burn might be able to see the wilderness even if the Old Ones tried to stop them."

Crow flapped his wings and began to preen in a nervous way, finally muttering, "Nevermore," and falling stubbornly mute.

Little Fur waited anxiously for Brownie's next visit, hoping the pony would snort in scorn as he often did when she reported some wild tale of Crow's. Indeed, she counted on his laughing and explaining how Crow had gotten it wrong. But Brownie only said, "I am sure that the other humans will catch the tree burners before long."

"Catch them?" Little Fur asked, confused.

"The tree burners are rogue humans," said Brownie. "The other humans are angry at them because every time they light a fire, the wind carries seeds of flame to human houses and they burn down as well as the trees. Last night fire jumped into one of the high houses. If you sniff you will smell the smoke from it still, for the other humans have not managed to put it out yet."

"Why are the tree burners doing it?" Little Fur wondered.

"No one knows. They wear masks and keep themselves secret," Brownie said. "Lots of humans are worried about the trees and are sleeping in parks to protect them."

"*Humans* want to protect trees?" Little Fur asked, wondering if she had heard rightly.

"I told you all humans are not bad."

"All humans *stupid*," Crow muttered.

"Even if the tree burners do come this far, the Old Ones won't let them come here," Brownie assured her.

"If a fire is lit in the pony park, the *flames* will come here."

There was a grim silence, and then Crow fluttered down. "Crow knowing what to do. Must asking advice of Sett Owl. Many animals asking Herness to thinking for them."

Little Fur clapped her hands. "Crow, you must

fly at once and ask her what we should do."

Crow ruffled his feathers evasively. "Herness not answering Crow."

"But you said she is used to being asked for advice by creatures other than owls."

"Answering all creatures *but* crows," said Crow. "Sett Owl hating crows because flock attacking her when she being fledgling. Maybe you can asking some other bird to talking her."

Little Fur shook her head. "Most wild birds can't remember anything for more than a few seconds unless it has to do with nesting or food. If only there was someone else I could ask, but all of the animals here are . . ."

"Too stupid," Crow concluded.

"Too small. I wonder if I could ask one of the other birds to invite the Sett Owl here," Little Fur murmured. "One of them might manage that."

"She not coming," Crow warned. "She flying bad because of wing injured in attacking long ago. All wanting answers must coming to Herness in beaked house."

Brownie broke in to announce that he had to go home. Crow fluttered into a tree and tried to look as if he were thinking deeply, but he was bird enough for it to be hard for him to keep his mind on the problem. After all, his wings would lift him above any danger. He preened himself surreptitiously and soon fell asleep.

Little Fur lay wide awake in her favorite sleeping place among the roots of the eldest of the Old Ones. She had seen a fire only once, when lightning had struck at the edge of the wilderness, but rain had put it out before long. But the hot orange tongues of flame had traveled with frightening speed and she vividly remembered the whispered terror of the trees.

When at last she did sleep, it was an uneasy doze in which she seemed to hear the Old One whispering to her that all things came to an end, even seemingly immortal trees, and that fire was as much a force of nature as rain or sunlight or even humans.

Little Fur woke with tears on her cheeks and the knowledge that she must go to the Sett Owl. She climbed to the top of the hill and gazed outward, over the shadowy rooftops of the human dwellings around the wilderness to the mysterious, shining high houses in the distance. Animals said there were few trees and green places around the high houses, but the beaked house was in an older part of the city where roads were sometimes made from round cobblestones that let the earth breathe, and where there were trees and tiny parks and paths of grass. There were even green places where humans did not bother to go. Little Fur felt sure that she could make her way carefully from one of these green places to the next without losing touch with the flow of earth magic. And it could not be very far if, as Crow said, the bells they sometimes heard tolling in the wilderness belonged to the beaked house. She would have to go slowly but she could travel at night, when most humans slept. That meant a greater chance of encountering trolls, but there were not so many in the parts of the city where green things grew, and if she was careful, she could avoid them.

A greater risk would be the ragged, wrong-smelling humans that cats called greeps. There were a good many of these living in shallow burrows and crevices in the older parts of the city, and they were bolder than trolls because they were not afraid of other humans. But Little Fur had the impression from cats' tales that greeps were awkward and clumsy, so perhaps they could be avoided, too.

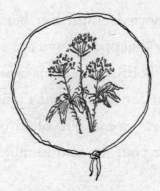

CHAPTER 3
A Dark Road

"This is a very bad idea," Brownie said.

"There is no other way." Little Fur pushed some dried mushrooms into her pouch.

"What if a human sees you?" asked Brownie. "You will be captured and put in a cage."

"You just jealous because it not being your idea that she seeking advice of Sett Owl," Crow crowed.

Brownie glared at him. "Birdbrain! It will be your fault if humans or greeps get her, and what about bad trolls?"

"I will flying ahead to warning her of danger-fulness," Crow boasted.

Brownie snorted. "Little Fur, have you thought about what will happen if you are seen?"

Little Fur softly patted his nose. "Don't be angry with me for doing what I must."

The stiffness went out of Brownie. "I am frightened for you," he said humbly. "I wish this were over."

"So do I," Little Fur said. She threw a fine gray spiderweb cloak about her and gave him a final hug. Then she turned to the two cats who had agreed to help guide her. Both were street cats that she had healed more than once, several times from battles with one another. Ginger was gray-furred, tough and silent, with orange eyes. Sly was lean and mean, with one narrow green eye and a broken tail tip. Crow had fetched them when Little Fur suggested it might be good to have scouts on the ground as well as one on the wing.

"Let's go," Sly hissed.

"What about the Old Ones?" Brownie called out to Little Fur as Crow took to his wings. "Have you told them what you are doing?"

"They will know," Little Fur said, and she set off in the direction that Crow had taken, flanked by the two cats.

Little Fur stared in dismay at the black road stretched before them, thinking that it was like a river of cat shadow which, if crossed, would permit no return. Yet they must cross it, for the beaked house lay on the other side.

"Can't crossing here," Crow said. He was perched on the high, thin wooden barrier separating the black road from the grassy common they had crossed. "Must going on grass path until reaching tunnel under road."

Little Fur stepped gingerly through the gap in the wooden barrier onto the sparse grass path that ran by the black road. Earth magic flowed through it, but so sluggishly that after a few steps, Little Fur decided she must try to help it.

She dropped to her knees and opened her seed pouch. Choosing three seeds of a hardy, long-rooted ground creeper that would like the dry, sandy earth better than grass, she pushed them into the dirt, covered them and dribbled some water from her bottle over them. If the seeds germinated, the creeper would spread swiftly along the verge, and eventually the wind would carry its seeds to the other side of the road. And where green things grew well, they would summon the earth spirit more strongly.

Suddenly Ginger hissed, "Quick! Road monster coming!"

There was nowhere to hide, so Little Fur flung herself down on her face and pulled her cloak over her head. For a long moment, there was nothing but the dusty smell of the weary earth

under her cheek. Then the ground began to tremble and she heard the unmistakable snarling growl of a road beast. She had heard them in the wilderness, but this was so much louder.

When she could bear it no longer, she peeped out and saw it coming along the black road at a tremendous speed: an enormous, flat-sided beast like no creature she had ever seen. It moved on great black wheels and its eyes were bulbs of glaring white. Without warning, it gave a scream-ing cry. Little Fur pressed her face to the dirt and felt all the hair prickle up on her neck as it passed, sucking the air after it and lifting the dry earth into a gritty whirlwind in its wake. When she dared to look after it, the road monster's red back-eyes were staring at her. But it did not turn or stop.

It took Little Fur a long while to be able to stand. Ginger sat on his haunches watching her and she wondered that he could be so calm.

"Let's going," Crow cawed, wheeling above.

Little Fur nodded, but the truth was that she wanted to go as fast as she could back to the wilderness and never leave it again. Yet what would become of the Old Ones if she did? Sly had vanished, and as they set off again, Little Fur wondered if the road monster had frightened her away. She would not blame Sly if it were so.

When the road began to curve, the wooden barrier curved, too, and Little Fur could no longer see ahead. So it was a shock when she came abruptly to the end of the grass path. Ahead, the black road now ran alongside the high wooden barrier with only a narrow gray curb to separate them. Before Little Fur could call out to Crow, Ginger stretched out a scarred gray paw to dab at a line of grass pushing up between the gray curb and the black road.

Little Fur touched one toe to the narrow seam of grass and was surprised to find earth magic flowing along it. Trying not to think about what would happen if the road monster returned, she put her whole foot down over the seam, then gasped. "The road is hot!"

"The blackness holds the heat of the day."

Little Fur looked up to find Sly draped elegantly along the top of the wooden barrier. She rose and leaped lightly down to sniff at the surface of the black road. "Nice and warm to lie on, but dangerous," she purred, as though the thought of being in danger pleased her.

Little Fur set off along the grass seam, holding out both arms for balance and hoping it would not be long before there was a better place to walk.

By the time Little Fur reached another grass path, she was tired out. *How can being careful and anxious be so wearying?* Ginger was padding along tirelessly beside her, but Sly had gone ahead again. *Hunting,* supposed Little Fur.

All at once, she caught the scent of a tree and cast about until she saw it; small, with sparse foliage, it was growing beside one of the poles that held up glowing balls of false light. Little

Fur went to the tree, eager to touch its bark. Like most trees planted since humans had come, it was deeply asleep, but when she leaned her cheek against the trunk its dreaming came to her partly as words, partly as a humming vibration and partly as pictures that flashed into her mind.

Pity gripped her when she realized that the tree believed it was the only one of its kind. She might have tried to convince it that there were others, but what use would that have been when none were near enough to give it company? Instead, she rummaged in her pouch for a small tree orchid wrapped in leaves. She always carried one of these with her because their pollen was useful for healing inflammations in flesh as well as in bark. "You must be a friend to this tree now," she whispered to the orchid, pushing it into a leafy elbow of the tree where it would be safe from the bruising wind of the road beasts.

Crow landed on the lowest branch of the spindly tree. "Mustn't stopping here," he chided. "Must keeping on walking."

Little Fur smiled up at Crow. "How far is it to the tunnel that goes under the road?"

"Many wingflaps," Crow said.

Little Fur sighed. Crow couldn't count, so to him, millions and hundreds and dozens all meant the same thing: many.

They continued along the black road until Little Fur's head rang with its thick, unpleasant smell. She was very relieved when Crow cried out that the tunnel was just ahead. But to her dismay, it turned out to be a pipe going under the road.

Fortunately, there was earth at the bottom of it, where weeds and small plants had taken root.

"No trolls," Crow said, misunderstanding her hesitation.

The tunnel did not smell of troll. It did not even smell of humans, although it was clear that humans had made it. "What is it for?" she asked.

"After rains, water gushing through here," Crow said. "I going now. Waiting on other side."

"What about Ginger?" Little Fur worried. Sly had not long ago reappeared smelling of blood, and that was when the big gray cat had vanished.

"He will follow our scent when he has eaten," Sly said languidly.

"Going quickly," Crow ordered, taking to his wings.

CHAPTER 4

The Feeding of Beasts

It was dark in the tunnel but the troll part of Little Fur felt safe and her eyes adjusted quickly. Wet green algae coated the inside of the pipe, so that even if the dirt underfoot ran out, she would be able to keep touch with the flow of earth magic. As she walked, she bent to tweak leaves from a plant she had not seen before. But her thoughts were not on herbs so much as the road passing overhead.

"Why do humans make black roads?" she murmured.

"To summon road beasts,"
Sly said, looking back
over her shoulder.
"They keep them
as pets. I myself
have seen humans
bathing their
shells with water."

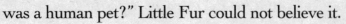

"The giant beast
that roared past us
was a human pet?" Little Fur could not believe it.

"Perhaps not that one," Sly admitted. "No
doubt there are road beasts that will not be tamed,
just as there are cats who will not be tamed."

"Truly, humans are strange," Little Fur mused,
still not sure whether to believe the cat.

When they emerged from the tunnel, the moon's
eye had opened and it peered narrowly down
at them. Crow said they must go back along
this side of the black road in order to reach the
beaked house.

Ginger appeared and took his place at Little Fur's side as she set off with a heavy heart, and Sly roamed ahead, as she seemed to prefer. But she returned almost at once, hissing that she could smell humans.

"Can we go another way?" Little Fur asked.

"No other way," Crow said.

They went on until Little Fur could smell humans, too, and she trembled at the thought that she was to see them at last.

The wooden barrier turned suddenly and ran around a square, flat field upon which stood a human dwelling spilling light out into the night from all sides. Little Fur gagged at the smell.

"That smell comes from the brew humans feed to road beasts," Sly said. "See? There is a road beast waiting to be fed under the wings of the place."

She was right. A black road ran in a loop from the main road around the building. One of the great, ugly road monsters stood on it, next to the bright house. It was so silent that it must have

41

fallen asleep. It did not look dangerous now, but Little Fur wondered what there was in such a thing for humans to love. It did not smell of kindness or softness or sweetness. It did not smell like it needed anything or loved anything. Indeed, it did not smell alive at all.

Crow flapped down to the grass beside her. "Not standing here! Humans will seeing you!" he cawed. "Going along barrier to broken place. Going very fastly."

But before Little Fur could move, the sleeping road beast suddenly roared to terrifying, deafening life and its dreadful eyes shot out beams of blinding whiteness that fell on all of them. Crow gave a squawk of fright and took to the air and the cats covered themselves in cat shadow.

Little Fur could not move. She felt as if the eyes of the road beast had a power that bound her, just as a snake holds its victims with the magic of its deadly gaze.

"Fly!" screeched Crow from overhead. When she did not move, he swooped down and raked

her head with a claw. The pain woke Little Fur from her trance and she turned to run. The road monster shrieked in rage. Little Fur fell to her knees and waited for it to rush at her and kill her. But nothing happened except that its roar grew louder. She opened her eyes and was amazed to see that instead of coming at her, the road beast was swerving away toward the black road!

It occurred to her that perhaps the road beasts *could not leave* the black roads.

She would have told this astonishing thought to Sly, but three humans ran out of the shining house. Little Fur stared at the sight of them, for all three were as pale as new mushrooms, and so big!

"They see you!" Sly hissed.

Little Fur realized it was true, and terror filled her. She sped along the barrier, her ears turned back to track the thud of the humans' feet. Sly disappeared through a gap in the fence and Little Fur followed, but there was a dry tangle of grass clogging the gap and she tripped and sprawled onto her hands and knees on the stone-studded ground.

"Get up!" Ginger rasped from his shadows.

Little Fur was too frightened to move. There was a long silence and then a big, round human head rose above the barrier.

She froze, for animals always said that humans had trouble seeing you when you stayed very still. One of the humans spoke and she caught the sweet scent of curiosity in its words. Another of the humans answered and its words were saturated with the hot, biting stink of cruelty. The head above the fence vanished and the voices faded.

Little Fur sat up. Her head hurt where Crow had scratched it, and her hands and knees burned where she had grazed them, but she had no time to treat her wounds. She wanted to get as far away from the beast feeding place as she could.

Sly and Ginger emerged from cat shadow close by. "Let's go," Sly said.

Little Fur obeyed, knowing there was nothing else to do but go on.

They crossed a stony field and climbed through a little ditch which brought them to a green paddock where earth magic flowed strongly. The grass had been well cropped by a flock of white animals and seeing them made some of the fright leak out of Little Fur. Four-legged and white-furred, the animals had delicate horns and cloven hooves. Little Fur would have liked to speak with them, but Crow was overhead screeching at her to hurry.

On the other side of the field was a small stand of pear trees. They had been planted in the human fashion, in neat, unnatural rows, and the field smelled of humans, but their scent was half smothered by the smell of pear nectar. Little Fur went to the nearest tree and put her face against its lichen-dappled bark. She soon learned that it had been planted by a human who came often to harvest its fruit. A tiny, drab bird nesting on one of its branches told Little Fur that the harvesting human came in daylight. The only humans that came at night were greeps who would sometimes stumble to the foot of a tree and fall down to sleep, reeking of their strange appetites.

Little Fur shuddered and was about to turn away when a thought came to her. She touched the tree again and sent a picture of humans burning trees into its dreams, and the sense of her own quest to save the Old Ones. A great shiver of sadness went through it and two pears dropped fatly to the ground.

Little Fur felt sick because even this tree, deeply asleep as it was, knew of the tree burners.

"It wants you to take its seeds," the bird told her, hopping to a lower branch and fixing its tiny, fierce eyes on her.

Little Fur picked up the fruit, wondering if the tree wanted her to plant its seeds in the wilderness. She laid her hand against the tree one last time, and promised that its seeds would be safe with her. Then she bade the bird farewell and left.

The pears in her arms grew heavy. She ate one as she walked, pushing its dark, sticky seeds into a little pocket at the hem of her tunic. She took some twine from her bag to fasten the other pear to her back. They crossed an overgrown field where there were many bare, dead patches of earth. The flabby coldness of that dead earth filled her with revulsion and pity. Occasionally, she would find a patch that was not quite dead; then she would stop, despite Crow's objections, and push a seed from her pouch into the ground.

At length they came to another of the barriers so beloved of humans, and Little Fur suddenly remembered that Brownie called them fences. This one was no more than low posts of wood driven into the ground with metal strings stretched between them. The real barrier was a thick, high hedge growing beside it, but she could easily crawl under both.

She was on her hands and knees when she caught the strong smell of humans on the night air.

"Better not to think so much," Sly advised. "The smell of fear thoughts is strong."

"You think humans could smell me?" Little Fur asked in horror.

"Humans can't smell, but trolls can," Sly answered. "If they smell your fear, they will come to see if what is so frightened is also small and tasty. Better to think of nothing."

Little Fur did not know how to think of nothing, but perhaps she could think of something that did not make her frightened, like lying on one of the hill meadows in the wilderness, watching the clouds. Before she could try, however, bells began to toll.

CHAPTER 5
Still Magic

Little Fur gazed through a barrier of metal spikes at the enormous, misshapen stone dwelling which Crow assured her was the beaked house. It was the queerest building she had ever seen. Set in the middle of a stone-paved yard, it was tall in some places and low in others, wide in parts and narrow in other parts. There were sections where the walls went suddenly in or out or had been made to bulge into round shapes. It was tall, but not as tall as the high houses, and rather than being flat-topped as they were, it had a peaked roof. One part of the roof rose steeply from the rest, like a bird's beak, which had given the house its name. There were even two small sticks fixed at the tip as if a great bird were carrying twigs to its nest. This ought to have made it look silly, but somehow the beaked house had a grave, still air that made Little Fur feel grave and still, too.

"What do humans do here?" she wondered.

"They sing," Sly said.

"Humans *sing*?" Little Fur was astonished.

"Humans singing very badly," Crow cawed, hopping neatly from the top of one spike to another. "Not like Crow."

"Are there any humans here now?" Little Fur asked quickly, knowing how very loud and bad Crow's singing was. "I mean, I suppose one of them must have rung the bells."

Instead of answering, Crow fixed Little Fur with a stern look. "Cats cannot going with us now. Sett Owl not liking cats."

"I like owls," Sly said. She sat on her haunches and began to lick one paw daintily.

"Will you wait here for me with Ginger, please, Sly?" Little Fur pleaded. "The Sett Owl might refuse to speak with me if you come. And, Crow, it might be better if you don't come in either."

Crow gave an affronted croak. "Well, then. If Crow not being wanted . . ."

"Oh, Crow, please don't be difficult." Little Fur reached up to touch his feathers.

She found a gate in the spiked barrier. A chain of heavy metal loops held it shut but she could slip through the gap. Little Fur stepped gingerly onto the cobblestones and was relieved to feel earth magic flowing under and between them.

She crossed the yard to the beaked house and began searching for niches and ledges where an owl might roost. There were patches of a pale unknown moss growing over the wall and she stopped to take a little piece for her pouch. When her fingers accidentally brushed the wall, she gasped in shock, for she had felt the tingling touch of magic, *only it was not earth magic.*

Heart pounding, she reached out again and put her finger on the bare stone. Again she felt it. A strange, still magic potent enough to make the hair stiffen on her neck. It felt how earth magic might feel if it were to build up in a great pool behind a dam. But Little Fur had no feeling that this power would ever overflow. It was as if the beaked house were a bottomless vessel.

The wind suddenly gusted to life, making

her cloak and hair billow and snap, and all at once the air was filled with the strange and mysterious scents of the world outside the wilderness.

Little Fur caught a flutter of movement on a ledge jutting out from the wall above her.

"Pigeon," she called softly. She smelled that the bird did not want to answer her, but it could not ignore her since she had called it by kind. At last it came out and she saw that it was a young pigeon with pretty pink-and-gray speckled feathers and a bright gaze.

"Crooo! Who is calling pigeon?" asked the pigeon. Its words had the same scrambled quality that Little Fur found in all bird minds, but unlike Crow's voice, there were no shadings to suggest a deeper intelligence.

"I call," Little Fur said slowly. "I have come far to ask the advice of the Sett Owl. Do you know where she roosts?"

"Crooo! What being important to you may not being so to Sett Owl," the pigeon warned. "What question would you asking?"

Little Fur answered politely that her question could only be told to the Sett Owl because it was so difficult and complicated. She crossed her fingers, hoping that this pigeon would be as scatterminded as those she had healed in the wilderness.

"Complicatings," sighed the pigeon. "Crooo! What is pointiness of making things so?"

"Some things just *are* complicated without anyone making them so."

"That being truthfulness," the pigeon admitted. It puffed out its chest in sudden decision. "Above great doors is round hole with torn metal web. There can you getting in to see Herness."

"The Sett Owl roosts *inside* the beaked house?" Little Fur was dismayed, for how could she get to the Sett Owl without losing touch with the flow of earth magic?

The pigeon smelled her disappointment and misunderstood it. "Crooo! You are having winglessness. Very inconvenient. But there being another way into beaked house for creeping things."

Little Fur did not much like being called a creeping thing, though perhaps it was a fair description from a bird's point of view. She doubted that she would be able to use this other entrance either, but she might as well go and look at it.

It did not take her long to find the opening, which was a square of darkness at the base of the stone wall bathed in moonlight. To her delight, it was the mouth of a tunnel that ran under the wall, so its base was made of good earth. Her moon shadow knelt beside her on the wall as she sniffed. The smell of the strange magic was much stronger here. As Little Fur crawled into the opening, she shivered, wondering if she would see the source of the still magic.

The tunnel was long because the walls of the beaked house were thick, but there was little to see other than mouse droppings and a few leaves caught in a tattered spider's web. As she came closer to the end, Little Fur began to smell human feelings all muddled together—weariness and sadness, despair and longing—but her nose also told her that there were no humans inside. It was as if they had found some way of leaving their feelings in a place even after they had left it. Brownie had never spoken of that, so perhaps it had something to do with the magic in the beaked house.

She poked her head out of the tunnel and it was like dipping into water, only it was not water but magic that lapped about her. Sitting back, Little Fur rubbed her tingling cheeks. There was just one great chamber in the beaked house. Long wooden benches faced a raised part of the floor at one end, where there was a table draped with a rich, sinuous cloth. Metal objects sat on it, gleaming in a false, red-tinged light. Huge stone vessels of cut lilies stood on either side of the table, filling the air with the melancholy scent of their dying. Little Fur was so lost in wonder at the queerness of it all that it was some time before she remembered to look for the Sett Owl.

Her troll vision made light of the shadows, but the room was vast and there were many corners. Little Fur looked for a long time but could not see the owl in any of them. The roof of the chamber mimicked the shape of the outer roof, so that one end went steeply up where the beak rose on the outside. There was a glimmer of gold in the gloom gathered at the tip, which must be the metal bells that had rung as they approached. No doubt they had been made to ring by one of the devices that humans were so clever at making to do things they could not or did not want to do.

But stare as she might, she could not see the Sett Owl up there either.

Leaning out of the tunnel as far as she could, Little Fur craned her neck to look along the wall. A giant stone shaped into the likeness of a human stared down at her, its face sternly sorrowful, as if she had done something very bad and it knew and pitied her for it. But the stone human had been made by humans, so the pity in its eyes must be meant for its own kind.

Little Fur was just beginning to wonder if she dared to shout out to the owl when there was a rough, scruffling sound behind her. A fat he-rat wriggled past her, muttering crossly.

"It is forbidden to block the way of other pilgrims," he snapped, turning to glare ferociously at her.

"Have you come to see the Sett Owl, too?" Little Fur asked.

"Certainly not! I serve Herness." The rat lifted his head so that he could look down his nose at her. "Do you have the proper payment?"

Little Fur was about to say she had nothing of value when she remembered the second pear. Untying it from her back, she found that it had gone to mush, but the smell of it was still good.

"You must carry it to the offering place." The rat pointed his twitching nose toward the raised part of the floor.

"I can't leave the tunnel," Little Fur said.

The rat sniffed. "Herness will not attack you."

"I'm not frightened of the owl," Little Fur said.

"But you must ask if she will come down here, so that I can ask my question."

"Certainly not!" huffed the rat. "Herness is too important to make house calls."

Little Fur had no idea what the rat was jabbering about, but she saw how his greedy eyes never left the pear, which was giving off the most delicious smell. Her own stomach rumbled, reminding her that she had not eaten for some time, and the rat bared his teeth. "Must not eat offering!" he hissed. "Sacreligion is forbidden."

Little Fur wondered why all of the creatures who lived close to humans talked such nonsense. "Ask the owl to see me, or I might as well have my supper."

The rat let out an anguished squeak and darted away.

Little Fur sat back on her heels and drank some water, calm because the worst of her journey was behind her. How Brownie would gasp to hear of her adventures! But perhaps he would be disappointed, too. His stories never told of being hurt or frightened or bruised during adventures.

There was a great fluttering of wings overhead and Little Fur leaned forward and looked up. An enormous owl was descending in a rush of air, her talons and wings outstretched.

CHAPTER 6
The Sett Owl

Little Fur cringed but the great owl merely landed heavily on the nearest wooden bench. One of her wings would not fold properly and hung down like a ragged cloak. The rat came running along the floor toward them, his toenails scratching against the flagstones. He stopped beside the pear, his eyes going from the fruit to Little Fur to the owl with crafty uncertainty.

Little Fur turned back to the owl, who regarded her with the same sternness as the stone statue had done. Little Fur said meekly, "Herness, here is my offering." The rat gave her a baleful stare, which puzzled her.

The owl chuckled. "Gazrak does not like it that you have insisted I come down. Usually he would eat the best of the offering and then bring what is left to me."

The rat squealed with indignation. "No, Herness! What filthy creature has been lying to you about me? Never would faithful Gazrak do such a low thing. Never." He sank to his belly, groveling.

The owl sighed. "Eat, Gazrak, but leave the seeds."

The rat abandoned his cringing, gouged a great, juicy chunk of the pear and darted away.

"He took the best bit," Little Fur said.

"He is a rat," the owl responded mildly. "Creatures generally behave as their natures dictate, unless there is something that causes them to do otherwise. Such as the threat to the wilderness from whence you came, Little Fur. Neither troll nor elf would normally make such a journey as you have undertaken."

Little Fur's mouth fell open. "How do you know who I am?"

"I often know who comes, because those who have sought my advice are sworn to bring to me

such news as I might find useful. It is part of the price they pay for failing to solve their own problems. And it causes those who come to feel the proper awe."

"I see," Little Fur said, though she didn't quite. "But if you like everyone to be in awe of you, why did you tell me how you knew I was coming?"

"One does not need to create the illusion of mystery when true mystery exists," the owl said. She fluffed herself up and then resettled. "I heard that an elf troll meant to come to see me. I knew of you because I have sometimes sent wounded creatures to you to be healed, or others to seek refuge in the enchanted wilderness of the Old Ones. I thought the rumor of your intention to journey here was nonsense. Then, from dusk yesterday, I began hearing reports from animals and birds who claimed you were moving through the city. I might still have thought it foolish gossip, but then the trees began to dream that Little Fur would vanquish the tree-burning humans. That she swore an oath."

Little Fur was aghast. "But I didn't!"

"Did you not take the seeds of a tree when it offered them?" the owl asked.

"I did, but only because it wanted me to plant them somewhere safe."

"Do you not know, Little Fur, that to take a seed freely given by a plant is to make a promise?"

"No . . . I didn't know that," Little Fur stammered, but immediately she realized that somewhere, deep down, she *had* known it. "I mean, I didn't understand what the tree was thinking. I only promised to plant the seeds somewhere safe."

"But where will be safe in a world where the tree burners have their way?" the Sett Owl asked gravely.

Little Fur's heart was beating very fast. "I can't stop the tree burners, Sett Owl. You know I can't. I am not a hero. Humans have chased me and a road monster tried to kill me as I was coming here and I would have been caught or killed if not for my friends. I only want to know how to protect the Old Ones. And if you can tell me that, then I can keep my promise to the pear tree."

"Is that all you would ask of me?" the Sett Owl said. The flecks in her eyes were star clusters in a dark sky and Little Fur had the oddest sensation that the unknown magic pooled in the beaked house was deepest around the Sett Owl.

"I don't know what you mean," she whispered.

"Would you not rather ask how you could save all of the trees?"

She licked her lips nervously. "I am only—"

"Only a small creature who undertook a difficult and dangerous journey with the help of a treacherous crow."

"Crow is—"

The owl's eyes flashed. "You came for my advice. Have the courtesy to listen to it! I cannot give you any power to save your wilderness. But I can tell you that unless the tree killers are stopped, the Old Ones will burn."

Little Fur's eyes filled with tears. "Why are the humans doing this?"

"The tree-killing humans are consumed with a desire for deadness and blackness. The seeds of destruction exist in all humans, but in the tree killers, that seed has flowered monstrously because of a potion given to a greep by the Troll King. At his command, the greep passed it on to the humans who became the tree burners."

Little Fur was shocked. Of all the answers she had imagined, not one was this. "Can . . . can the tree burners be healed?" she asked.

The Sett Owl looked at Little Fur for a long moment, her gaze cool and strange; then she said, "It is to your credit that you would think first of healing. But it is too late for the humans who have drunk the potion. Yet there may be a way to save the Old Ones and all of the other trees as well."

"How?" Little Fur asked eagerly.

"You must travel three days toward the high houses, and then turn your steps toward the place where the sun will open its eye. Go in that direction until you come to the burying place of humans. Beyond is a wood, and in that wood is a deep crack in the earth. Humans do not go there, for within it sleeps an ancient power that turns their minds and eyes away."

"An Old One?" Little Fur asked in delight.

"I do not know what form the power takes," the owl said. "But whatever sleeps there has done so since the first age of the world. Some say that the earth spirit flowed from its dreams."

"Will you ask it to help us?" Little Fur said in a small voice. Her heart was beating fast, for she feared that she knew the answer and dreaded it.

"You came to me to learn how the trees may be saved. I tell you this: if you would stop the tree burners, you must go into the crack and awaken the sleeper," the owl said implacably. The flecks in her eyes seemed to whirl and Little Fur felt that it was no longer just the owl with whom she was speaking, but something greater and vastly stranger.

"Are . . . are you the earth spirit?" she asked softly.

70

"No," the Sett Owl answered. "But in this place where power lies in a deep, secret pool, I am more than owl. Little Fur, understand that it is not only the life of thousands of trees at stake. If the tree burners are not stopped, they will keep burning until the flow of earth magic dies in this city. Then will the trolls make it a place of such dreadful power that a darkness ravenous enough to entirely devour the earth spirit will rise from it. That is the heart of the Troll King's desire."

"Herness, please, isn't there someone else who can go to this chasm? Someone strong and brave?"

"The task of thwarting the Troll King has been appointed to you, Little Fur," the owl said. "Will you accept it?"

Little Fur was trembling but she said, "Herness, I do not know how I can succeed. But if you say that I must, then I will go."

The owl blinked its lambent eyes, just once. "So then it is true. The sum is greater than its

parts." Her eyes closed and Little Fur heard a
gentle snore.

The Sett Owl had fallen asleep!

CHAPTER 7
The Making of Promises

"I promised," Little Fur told the others. They were all sitting under a tree growing just outside the spiked fence around the beaked house.

Crow cawed doubtfully. "Sounding farsome to this burying place."

"Three nights of going toward the high houses," Sly added. "That is outside my territory."

"What if sleeping power not wanting to be waking?" Crow said.

"I must find a way to wake it," Little Fur said.

"Must?" Ginger murmured.

Little Fur sighed. "What is the use of coming so far for advice if I won't follow it?"

"That is a sensibleness," Crow conceded.

"I don't know if it is sensible or foolish," Little Fur said wearily. "Will you come with me?"

"Crow coming," Crow said at once.

Sly rose sinuously, stretching herself out so that the bones in her spine cracked loudly. "I will hunt now," she said, and mantled herself in cat shadow.

"Soon the sun will open its eye," Ginger said. "You should find a place to rest for the day."

"Crow not tired," Crow complained.

"Then fly back and tell Brownie what has happened," Little Fur told him. "Hang my seed pouch around your neck and ask the rabbits to fill it again while you are there. But come back before the sun closes its eye again. And be careful."

"Crow having more carefulness than any other creature," Crow declared solemnly. He fluffed his feathers in readiness to fly, saying, "I telling Brownie we going on long terribleness of a journey." He flapped into the air before Little Fur could beg him not to exaggerate so poor Brownie wouldn't worry himself sick.

Then she thought uneasily that perhaps the dangers they would soon face could not be exaggerated.

She turned to look at the human high houses rising in the distance. At the top of the tallest, a green dome winked ceaselessly on and off. The color seemed a good omen, but the land between it and the beaked house was a jumbled mystery of low human buildings and black roads, and who knew what dangers lurked there. Yet the owl had said that the task was appointed to her, so there must be some hope of fulfilling it.

"Sleep," Ginger said, padding up beside her on velvet paws. "You stink of tiredness and tangled thoughts."

75

Little Fur climbed high enough into the tree that no passing human would catch sight of her and curled against the trunk. She had a leaf-scalloped view of the beaked house, and behind it, the dark blue sky arched down to a pink seam of light opening up at the horizon.

As she slept, Little Fur was drawn so deeply into the tree's dreaming that she became the tree. A fragrant spring wind rattling softly at her branches teased tender shoots to life, making them unfurl. She sent a root into the damp earth, probing for a subterranean stream, and drank her fill of the pure water springing from the deep stream at the heart of the world.

She felt the sun on her leaves, turning them golden and then brown, and the small sorrow that was their falling. She dreamed of snow flying and of snow melting, and of sunlight again, wan and pale and then bright and hot.

The dream seemed to last years. It was compelling and full of interest, though nothing happened other than the changing of the seasons. Then the sky darkened and a dreadful storm tore up a tree that had once grown on the other side of the spiked fence. The tree crashed against the wall of the beaked house, cracking part of the stonework.

Little Fur woke with a thundering heart. She wondered if the beaked house and the still magic it contained had made her dream the tree's dream, for that had never happened before. She looked over to the beaked house and was startled to see that the doors were now ajar!

A human came out, its long black tunic snapping in the wind. It came across the cobbles and disappeared under the tree. Curious in spite of her fear, Little Fur crawled carefully to the end of the branch she had been sleeping on and peeped down. She could not see the face of the human, but she could smell the sour reek of its discontent as it gazed back at the beaked house. The smell strengthened when another human came out and turned to close the doors behind it.

It wore the same black tunic as the other, but its movements were stiff and slow and its hair white. The old human called out to the younger one, and there was so much kindness in its words that Little Fur was astonished. But when the younger human answered, its voice was full of cold, hard places and cutting edges. It made a sneering gesture at the tree and the moss-covered cobbles; the old human shook its head and made a gesture that embraced the beaked house and the tree and the cobbles. The younger human spoke again, its words soft and accepting, yet such hot waves of rage and greedy impatience burned off it that Little Fur wondered the old human did not recoil. It was clear to her that the younger human would do anything to get what it wanted.

Both humans went out through the gap in the spiked barrier, and Little Fur saw how the younger fretted at having to measure its step to the slow tread of the old human.

When they had gone, she climbed down.

She had slept away most of the day and the air was very warm, full of the drowsy hum of bees and the whirr of cicadas. She drank some water from her bottle, knowing that she must soon find a way to fill it. There was no sign of Sly or Ginger, but maybe the humans had shooed them away while she had been lost in the tree dream. Or they might be hunting for food before the journey. She did not want to think that they had decided to come no farther.

Crow's absence troubled her more. She thought he would have remembered to come, but he might have forgotten to hurry. To pass the time and stop herself from worrying, she set about gathering edible seeds from small plants growing in the grass about the tree, tucking them into the hem of her tunic.

Very soon the sun had closed its eye and the world fell into shadow. Little Fur decided that she had to go on. She knew that humans retreated into their dwellings when it grew dark, even if they did not sleep at once, and so if she was careful, she ought to be safe. If the others came after she had gone, they would know where to go, for she had told them all of the Sett Owl's instructions.

Leaving the cobbled yard and the beaked house, Little Fur struck out directly toward the high houses, but almost at once she came to another black road cutting across her path. There was nothing to do but to follow it and hope she would find a way to cross. She thought it would not be too hard, for this road was narrow and cracked along the edges. All she needed was a crack that ran from one side to the other.

The road soon brought her to a long row of human dwellings. There were lights in many of the windows, but Little Fur had no fear that she would be seen if a human glanced out, for the moon had not risen and there were bushes growing along the grass path where she could hide. Even so, she stopped often to sniff at the wind because she was alone now and must keep a watch for greeps and road beasts, as well as for bad trolls.

Little Fur walked for at least an hour seeing nothing more frightening than a rabbit, which ran away before she could speak to it. Then she came upon two lines of metal which cut across the grass path and ran over the black road to vanish into a lane on the other side. Wooden fences rose up on either side of the lane, hiding it from the human dwellings. Little Fur felt a surge of excitement, for it ran directly toward the high houses!

She knelt to look at the metal rails more closely and saw that grass grew along a gap in the black road. She stood and looked both ways along the black road. Not a single road beast had passed and she decided to take a chance.

Little Fur had gotten more than halfway across the road when her foot brushed one of the rails. It stung savagely. When she leaned close, her nose told her that something poisonous had been spilled along it. But the smell was old and the poison too weak to do more than cause her discomfort, so she forced herself to go on. When she got to the other side, she felt a burst of pride at having managed her first obstacle alone.

She followed the metal rails into the lane and sniffed. There was the merest trace of faded human scent, and trolls would not go there because of the earth magic flowing through the grass paths beside the rails. But Little Fur stayed alert, for this was just the sort of place where greeps might lurk.

She saw none, but she was relieved to reach

the end of the lane, for it took a long time and more than once she had heard human voices on the other side of the fences. The metal rails ran out of the lane and over a grassy field. She could see human dwellings around the edges of the field but they were far off, so she continued to follow
the rails.

Little Fur had walked for some time and was wondering what purpose the metal rails served when a gust of wind brought her the unmistakable perfume of ripe cherries. Her mouth watered, for she loved cherries almost as much as mushrooms.

There was not a single tree in sight but there was a stone wall a little distance off, and she guessed the cherry tree must be on the other side of it. She abandoned the rails and went to the wall. Clearly humans had built it, but it was a long time since they had bothered with it, for there was no human smell about it at all.

 The scent of cherries was stronger than ever and Little Fur was suddenly determined to get to them.

CHAPTER 8

An Attack!

"Don't ssstep on me or I will bite you," a voice said. Little Fur's heart gave a great lurch of fright. She had been so intent on the smell of cherries that she had not noticed an eroded hollow in the ground close by the wall. A green snake lay at the base of it, half inside its hole, watching her with bright yellow eyes.

"Greetings, Snake," she said politely.

The snake lifted its head off the ground, its eyes glowing. But Little Fur was careful not to look directly into its gaze. Snakes were always trying to hypnotize you even if you were too big for them to swallow. Seeing that she would not fall under its sway, the snake laid its head down again and hissed crossly, "Jussst don't tread on me. I am waiting to shed a ssskin and that wantsss great concentration."

"I won't," Little Fur promised. She found herself lingering because the snake was the first creature she had spoken to since Crow and the cats had left her the night before. It occurred to her that she ought to ask it about the human burying ground, even though snakes did not travel far or lift their heads up much from their own affairs.

"Humansss!" the snake sneered, its tongue flickering between sharp white fangs. "I do not like humansss. What have you to do with them?"

"Nothing," Little Fur said hastily, wrinkling her nose at the smell of its malice. "It is only that I am looking for a chasm near this burying place."

"I do not know where humansss bury one another," the snake told her, settling back down, its eyes growing cloudy.

"I wonder . . . is there any way to get under this wall? A tunnel or a hole?" Little Fur asked, catching the rich scent of cherries again.

The snake's eyes cleared. "Well," it said slowly, "there isss a broken place in the wall where you can ssslither through." It withdrew into its hole as Little Fur stood up.

She followed the wall around until she came to the broken place the snake had mentioned. It looked as if a giant hand had knocked it down a long time ago, for there were mosses and lichens growing all over it. She had no need to worry about where she stepped, for the earth spirit ran all around the stones. On the other side was a yard choked with long grass and bordered by high stone buildings. Their windows were as dark as blind eyes and she could see that the roofs had fallen in and some of the walls had holes in them. The smell of cherries was so strong now that Little Fur felt half drunk with it as she climbed over the crumbling wall.

The cherry tree grew in the deeper darkness between two of the ruined buildings, and she made her way over to it, struggling a little in the thick grass. She was quite close to the tree before she smelled the rotten, rancid sweetness of fermented fruit. It was too strong to be the result of windfall cherries, but she was hungry and did not stop to wonder what else might be causing it.

She reached out to take a great, fat, dark bunch of cherries from a trailing branch when something enormous and dreadful lurched out of the darkness behind it. Little Fur had never seen a greep, but she knew at once that a greep was what had caught hold of her arm. She had a horrifying

glimpse of its small, maddened eyes, barely visible in the great, filthy mass of wiry fur covering its head and chin; then it opened its mouth and the smell of its breath made her want to retch. It was a dreadful stew of rotting teeth and fruit and the rank stench of confused rage from the madness that had transformed it from human into greep.

Too late she wished she had remembered that animals always spoke of the rotten-fruit smell of greeps.

The greep loosened its grip slightly as it peered at her, and Little Fur wrenched her arm free. She might have gotten away but, as she turned, she tripped and fell. The greep was on her in an instant, this time closing a huge, hard hand about her ankle.

Little Fur went limp and closed her eyes. Feeling the creature's breath on her cheeks, she could smell its puzzlement and guessed that it was trying to decide what she was. It grunted and poked at her with its free hand. She made herself even more still, praying that the greep would think she was dead and let her go. But instead it kept hold of her and sat back, muttering to itself and giving out little bursts of crazed laughter.

It was silent awhile and then the greep muttered again to itself. Little Fur smelled troll in the words and remembered that the Troll King had given his potion to creatures like this—maybe even to this very greep! What if it decided to bring her to the Troll King?

Suddenly the greep began to struggle to its feet, and Little Fur realized that in another second it would stand and lift her into the air, severing her from the earth spirit forever. Desperately she struck out with her free foot, catching the greep in the belly. It grunted in pain and let her go. Little Fur scrambled to her feet and darted to the gap in the wall, ignoring the pain in her ankle.

She had almost reached the gap when the greep caught hold of her tunic. She yelped and tried to drag the cloth free but the greep grabbed her ankle again, this time twisting it cruelly. The pain was so great that Little Fur almost fainted.

The greep began to drag her back, but at that moment, a shadowy shape with flaring orange eyes leaped over the wall and landed claws first on the greep's head.

Ginger!

The greep gave a screech of shock and Little Fur was free. Sobbing with fear and pain, she

hauled
herself over
the mossy stones and
tumbled onto the grass on the other side of the
gap. Her legs would not hold her, so she dragged
herself along the ground to the hollow where
the snake had been lying and rolled into it. She
listened with a hammering heart to the greep's
roars and Ginger's savage battle cries. There was
the sound of running and of something heavy
falling, and suddenly Ginger gave a yowl of pain.
Then there was silence.

Little Fur prayed that nothing had happened
to him.

The greep clambered over the wall, cursing
and moaning and rubbing its head. Little Fur

lay very still. At last, the greep shook its fist at the sky and lumbered away in the direction from which Little Fur had come. Fearful of a trick, she did not move until it had gone completely out of sight. When she dared to go back into the yard where the greep had caught her, the smell of cherries was as strong as ever, but the thought of eating made her feel sick. She found Ginger lying by the wall, but her nose told her he was alive even before she felt the warmth of his body.

Ginger stirred at her touch and tried to rise.

"Rest," Little Fur said worriedly, smelling the cat's pain.

But he forced himself to get up. "We must go from here before the greep returns," he panted.

They had to help one another, for Little Fur was unable to put any weight on her hurt ankle and Ginger was dizzy and unsteady. Mindful that the greep would see them if it returned, Little Fur did not complain as they struggled along, angling away from the broken stone wall and back toward the metal rails. But Ginger did not turn to follow the rails as she had expected. He went over them and headed toward the human houses.

"Where are we going?" Little Fur asked, looking uneasily ahead.

"One of those human dwellings is empty. I sniffed it out when I was hunting. We can hide there."

His words were slurred and the moment they reached the fence separating them from the dwellings, he slumped sideways. Little Fur half fell with him, pain shooting through her leg as she leaned too hard on it. But her ankle was the least of her worries, for Ginger was losing blood. Disentangling herself, Little Fur turned to the fence and searched until she had found a spiderweb. Balling it up, she scraped up some earth, spat into it and worked it all into a sticky wad. She laid it over the gash on his flank and pressed it down hard, closing her eyes, the better to feel Ginger's spirit. It was strong, but there were torn places in it. Softly, she began to sing

them back together,
for she knew flesh could not
heal properly when the spirit was hurt. She could
not have said how long she sat there, singing and
pressing, but when she stopped, the moon was
looking down on them, waiting to see what would
happen next.

Little Fur's senses told her that the cat was
no longer in danger, and she lay down, falling at
once into a deep, exhausted sleep.

She dreamed that tree burners were chasing
her. They looked like greeps but they had yellow
snake's eyes and breathed a hot madness that
was strangely and horribly mingled with a sadness so deep and old that it was sweet and rotten

all at once, like fermented cherries. Little Fur tried to run, but she found that her feet had taken root. She stood there, helpless, as they encircled her, the hungry flames in their hands flickering in their eyes.

CHAPTER 9

The Mysteriousness of Humans

Little Fur was awakened by a weight on her chest. She opened her eyes to find Crow peering into her face, her pouch hanging around his neck.

"Crow!" she cried, lifting off the heavy pouch and hugging him. A sharp pain in her ankle reminded her of all that had happened the night before and she turned to find Ginger calmly licking at his wounds.

"You saved my life," she told him. "That greep would have—"

"Greep!" Crow squawked, flapping his wings in agitation. "Where being greep?"

"A greep caught me last night and Ginger rescued me," Little Fur explained. She tried to get up but the pain in her ankle was worse than the night before. Crow hopped away at her request to find a good, stout stick. She padded the top of it with her cloak and used it to help her hobble along. Ginger led them to a loose board in the fence, which they swung aside. A moment later they stood in one of the very small parks that humans liked to cultivate beside their dwellings. Gardens, Brownie called them.

The garden had a reassuringly wild and unkempt air, as if it had been left to its own devices for some time. Little Fur would have happily sat down where she was, but Ginger urged her on with the promise of a pond.

The pond lay in the merged shadow of two leafy trees. After they had all drunk from it, Ginger stretched out to sleep under one of the trees. Little Fur sat under the other and began to make a poultice for her ankle. If she could draw the swelling out, then sleep to replenish her spirit, she should be able to walk without the stick when they set off again.

"Did you see Brownie?" she asked Crow as she worked.

"Brownie in wilderness," he said. "He saying bravest of all creatures being Little Fur and Crow. Cats brave, too," he added with a sideways glance at Ginger.

"Did you hear anything of the tree burners?"

"They coming," Crow said darkly. "But Crow knowing where is human burying place. Starling telling Crow. I can showing the way."

"That's wonderful," Little Fur said. Then she had another thought. "Did you see Sly?"

"Sly not coming," Crow said.

Little Fur could not blame her. Cats were at a great disadvantage outside their territories. Look what had happened to Ginger. But without him, she would be dead or a prisoner of the trolls.

When she had finished the poultice, she lay down, resting her head on the root of the tree. She sent her mind into the tree, but rather than entering its dream, she was startled to find herself slipping through its roots into the flow of earth magic. She traveled where it went, and felt its delight as it surged strongly through green places where there were no humans to despoil them. It also took her to places where the earth had died, which looked to Little Fur like great gray holes with a howling black wind that whirled and hissed endlessly. Earth magic swirled around the rim of the dead places, unable to enter. Little Fur felt the earth magic's mourning as a song of strange and compelling beauty.

When she woke next, it was late afternoon and she was hungry. Her leg felt so much better that she wondered if it had been less hurt than she had imagined. But when she pulled the poultice away, the bruising was dark purple and tinged with yellow, as if days had passed since she had hurt it, rather than just a few hours.

Ginger was still sleeping, only now he was lying rather comically on his back with his paws poking up into the air. Crow slept, too, so Little Fur limped quietly away, determined to find food. She had not gone far when she caught the delicious, earthy smell of mushrooms! She soon found a patch growing under an overhanging bush, and sat down at once to gorge herself. There was no point in gathering any for the others because they did not eat mushrooms.

It was then that Little Fur caught sight of the human dwelling. She had learned a great deal about humans during her journey, but somehow instead of satisfying her, this only made her want to know more. For instance, how exactly did a human become a greep? Brownie said that they were humans who were broken inside, while

Crow claimed they were outcast humans, shunned by their kind and forced to live alone. Both Sly and Ginger said that they were rotten in the center, like a tree whose heartwood had gone black.

Little Fur came to the edge of a small grassy expanse, and gazed across it at the human dwelling. She knew that she ought to turn back, but she stepped from the long shadows into the sunlight and limped carefully over to a square of unmelting ice set in a gap in the wall of the dwelling. Part of her was amazed that she dared to do it, even though her nose told her there were no humans nearby. She wondered how Brownie would react when she told him what she had done. Then she smiled, thinking that she was as bad as Crow, admiring her own stories even before she told them.

She peered through the ice.

There was nothing at all inside. The humans who had lived here had taken all of their things with them when they went. Little Fur wondered

what had
made them
leave and where
they were now.
Animals only changed
dens or burrows because they had no choice,
but she supposed that creatures as powerful as
humans could do whatever they wanted to do.

She turned away reluctantly, realizing that the empty dwelling would answer none of her questions. Then her heart gave a great leap of fright, for sitting on the branch of a tree growing on the other side of the fence separating this dwelling from the next was a human! *And it was watching her!*

Little Fur expected it to scream or call out to other humans. But it only stared at her with wide eyes and an even wider mouth. Then the wind changed direction and she smelled it. The small human gave off a scent that was richer and lovelier than anything she had ever smelled! It was the scent of the Old Ones mixed up with the smell of Crow telling his stories, and of Brownie galloping. It was the smell of ripe cherries and mushrooms and rain on hot grass.

Enchanted, Little Fur found herself limping a few steps closer. The small human's lips curved into a smile of delight, and Little Fur realized with wonder that seeing *her* was making the human smell like this. She remembered then that one of the humans at the beast feeding place had given off a similar smell after seeing her, though that had faded at once when another of the humans had sneered at it.

The small human spoke and Little Fur knew that she ought to retreat, but something stopped her. Maybe it was the smallness of the human, or the longing in its voice, which woke an answering echo in her own heart, but she was on the verge of replying when she heard another human calling out.

The small human in the tree turned away to answer it, and Little Fur withdrew into shadows reaching like fingers across the grass. The small human turned back and its face fell. Little Fur could not see the other human, but it spoke and its words were full of tenderness and love, soured slightly by a bitter under-scent of disbelief.

The small human climbed down from the tree and Little Fur was horrified to smell herself in its words—her red hair and her ears and her bare feet. She listened anxiously, but the scent

105

of disbelief given off by the other human grew stronger, and the incredible sweetness of the small human began to fade.

Finally, Little Fur limped slowly back toward the pond, wondering how a small human such as this could grow up to be a greep. Was it something to do with the way the sour smell of disbelief swallowed the sweetness in it?

"Where have you been?" Ginger asked.

Little Fur jumped. "I went to look in the human house," she said. "I was curious."

"What did you learn from it?" asked Ginger.

"That humans are mysterious," she said.

CHAPTER 10
Underth

Back by the pond, they found Sly had arrived and was watching a big golden fish that nudged its head out into the air. Its scales glinted gold in the sunlight that dappled the pond now, and Little Fur thought it quite the loveliest thing she had ever seen. She could smell that Sly was hungry, but she could not help being glad that the fish was too wily to come close to the bank.

"I smell blood," the black cat said coolly, without taking her eye off the fish. In the tree overhead, Crow rustled his feathers but said nothing.

"A greep caught me," Little Fur told her, wanting to ask where she had been all this time, but she knew the black cat would not answer. "Ginger made it let me go."

"A pity he did not smell it before it caught you." Sly threw a mocking look at the gray cat.

"Ginger wasn't with me when the greep jumped out," Little Fur said, rather indignantly.

Suddenly they heard the long, distant scream of a creature so large that its passing, even at a great distance, made the earth shiver under Little Fur's feet. The surface of the pond rippled and shuddered, and the golden fish sank out of sight.

Crow erupted from the tree. "Thisaway!" he cawed. "Not goodly to be stopping here anymore. Let's going now!" He wheeled away and the others rose.

As they made their way through the garden, Little Fur asked Ginger if he knew what had made the sound.

"There are many things in the world," he said. They passed along the side of the empty human dwelling and through a smaller garden to the front fence of the place, which was low and made of stone. Beyond it was another black road bordered by grassy paths. There were several

109

small road beasts sleeping in a line by the side of the road which neither Crow nor the cats seemed to be troubled about. But passing by them, Little Fur could not help imagining that they would wake suddenly and turn their terrible, glowing eyes on her.

"Hurrying," Crow urged from above. "Big greenplace ahead."

The greenplace turned out to be an enormous, flat square of short grass bordered by black roads on three sides and human dwellings on the fourth. High, thin, metal-smelling devices stood on it in beds of sand where Sly said small humans came to play. Little Fur wondered what pleasure they would find in such a sad, bare place.

One of the metal devices made a loud creaking noise and Little Fur froze before realizing that it was only the wind that had made it move. Sly said that the metal objects were playthings for human younglings. One of them would sit on the little suspended bench that had made the creaking noise while a big human would push it to make it swing back and forth.

Ginger went to sniff at a bad-smelling metal container fastened to a wooden pole and Little Fur went to a big boulder balanced on its end in the ground, drawn by the smell of water. Water was trickling from the top of it and spilling down the side. Little Fur was about to drink when Crow gave a sudden urgent croak.

"Craaak! Humans coming!"

Heart racing, Little Fur pressed herself to the lump of stone.

"Be still," Sly warned. "Humans are always more interested in themselves than anything else. If you don't move, they won't even look this way."

But Ginger darted toward the humans and, to Little Fur's horror, planted himself firmly in front of them!

One of the humans stood back, folding its arms and shaking its head, but the other knelt and, to Little Fur's amazement, stroked Ginger slowly from head to tail. She waited for him to snarl and scratch, but he arched his back and gave every sign of enjoying the caress.

As the humans passed the big rock, Little Fur heard their words, which smelled of wisdom but also of nonsense. "What were they talking about?" she wondered aloud.

"Humans like the sound of their voices," Sly said. "They don't know what they are saying."

Little Fur did not think this was entirely true. But Ginger joined them and she thanked him shyly, thinking that this was the second time he had put himself in danger for her sake.

"Enough of resting," Crow declared. "We should going."

They passed through another lane and came to yet another black road. Little Fur was beginning to realize that black roads ran in a maze through the city and dreaded to think how many more they must cross. Then they came to a part of the city where there were neither trees nor grass paths, and where the human houses were higher and wider than they had been, and smelled of many inhabitants.

"I can't walk there," Little Fur protested.

"Must walking cracks in gray path," Crow urged. "Must going thisaway!"

"What if a human comes along?"

"Crow will flying and pecking at it," Crow said fiercely.

So Little Fur crept from one crack to the next, praying that no human would come from its dwelling. Yet when one did, she was amazed that it seemed not to see her, though she was quite close and passing through a circle of false light. Sly had been right in saying they saw little out-side their own doings.

It seemed an eternity before they came to a cobbled lane, which Crow said they should enter. Little Fur nearly wept with relief to feel earth magic flowing sturdily under the moss-rimmed stones. The lane brought them to a cobbled street where there were rows of human buildings so wide and square that they seemed like walls of buildings running along either side of the street. A queer, cold, metal-sulfur stink flowed from them, and Little Fur thought how practically everything humans built smelled bad. There must be something in their human lives that killed their sense of smell, because after living with them, animals and birds also seemed to lose their proper nose for things.

There were a lot of square, dark openings in the walls of the buildings and Little Fur tried not to feel that humans were peering malevolently from them.

"Humans not living here," Crow said. "They coming here only to making a muchness of noise and bad smells." Little Fur grew alarmed at this, but Crow added, "Not coming when moon watching."

"Fewer humans equal more greeps and trolls," Ginger muttered.

Occasionally the long, smooth walls of the buildings gave way to small stone houses that smelled very old. Little Fur guessed that a lot of these stone dwellings had been pushed down to make way for the new square buildings. Humans seemed to be always knocking down things they had made to build new things.

Crow flapped down to a narrow lane running between two of the big houses and instructed them to go that way, but Little Fur stopped, suddenly profoundly uneasy.

"What is it?" Ginger asked in his rumbling voice.

"I don't know," Little Fur admitted. Her nose could detect nothing in the lane, yet her instincts clamored that danger lay in this direction.

"Must going thisaway or must going back and back," Crow said firmly.

Little Fur did not know what to say. Everything in her resisted entering the lane but she could not say why. After another long, fruitless bout of sniffing, she decided that some forgotten memory must be prompting her fears. She took a deep breath and entered the lane. Halfway along it, she began to smell a horrible, sharp odor that grew stronger as they walked.

Sly had stopped by a square opening at the base of the wall of one of the big houses, and Little Fur realized this was the source of the hideous smell.

"Troll hole," Sly murmured.

Little Fur stared into the opening. The darkness filling it seemed as dense and sticky as syrup. Yet she could not detect the unmistakable hot reek of troll.

"Troll not being here," Crow remarked scornfully, strutting to the opening and poking his beak in. "Faugh! Some horrible human doing is down here."

"Humans have used it, but it's an old troll hole," Sly said. "It leads to Underth, but trolls don't bother with it because they have better and quicker ways to get there now."

Little Fur would have liked to ask Sly how she knew such things, but Ginger had stiffened and the fur on his neck was standing up in a thick ruff.

"Greep," he breathed.

"If greep coming, we must going." Crow flapped into the air and glided down the lane.

"I am not afraid," Sly sneered.

"I will scratch its eyes out." She sounded as if she would quite like a greep to come along, and when Little Fur and Ginger hurried after Crow, she lingered by the opening to the troll hole grooming her fur!

When Sly caught up with them a little time after, her long tail curled around Little Fur's neck in a dangerous sort of caress.

The lane brought them out of the big houses and back to the small stone dwellings. These were older than the others, for some of the roofs had fallen in and many of the openings and doors in them were closed up with wooden planks. Before Little Fur could ask why humans had abandoned them, she smelled smoke in the air. It was just a hint, but it made her think of the tree burners, and a wave of fear for the Old Ones crashed over her. Little Fur mastered her panic and told herself that no matter what the Sett Owl said, the Old Ones were powerful and had great resources. Perhaps at the last, the earth spirit itself would rise up through them and stop the tree burners, though that would not help the pear trees or the little sapling by the black road, nor all of the other millions of trees growing throughout the city.

Little Fur sighed, her heart sore and heavy in her chest. Thinking of the Old Ones was like pressing on a hurt place. The pull to go back to the wilderness was suddenly as strong as if she were connected to it by a real vine that was being tugged hard. As if conjured by her longing, she saw a tree growing ahead close by a stone wall. Little Fur's skin prickled because she could feel how the earth spirit surged toward it, yet as she came nearer, she saw that all of the branches on one side of the

tree were black and withered.

CHAPTER 11
The Dogness of Dogs

At one time the tree must have been healthy, for its massive, snaking roots had pushed the cobbles awry. Moss and small plants continued to grow thickly in the cracks, which proved that the tree had not been poisoned, as Little Fur had feared. She laid her hands on its much-scarred trunk only to find that its heartwood was rotten. There was nothing she could do, but she went deeper, striving to find a reason for the disturbance of the earth magic that she sensed surrounding the tree.

To her astonishment, she found *herself* in the tree's dream, sitting in the dense shade of the Old Ones, sorting seeds! The tree must have taken her image from the flow, and of course that was the answer to why the flow was agitated. The tree was responding to her appearance!

Sly began hissing like a snake. Little Fur turned to see her gazing malevolently along the street where the wall gave way to a queer fence of thin metal strands woven into a great web. This stretched as far along the street as they could see, and on the other side of it was a nasty-smelling huddle of wooden dwellings.

"What is the matter with her?" she whispered to Ginger.

"Dog," he said.

Little Fur's heart began to race. She had never seen a dog, but almost as many animals and birds had been hurt by dogs as by humans and trolls. Each one of them described the fearsome beasts quite differently, so that Little Fur knew they must have shape-changing blood in them.

The worst thing of all about dogs was their complete devotion to their human masters. It was even said that dogs would kill at a human's command.

Sly padded over to the tree and said softly, "The dog has smelled us but it does not know that *we* have smelled *it*." Her green eye glittered with triumph.

"Will it come after us if we turn back?" Little Fur asked. They could climb the tree to escape the dog's brutal teeth, but then they would be trapped there until its master came.

Before either cat could answer, the dog began to howl. Little Fur clapped her hands over her ears at the sound, which seemed to tear the night. Crow fluttered onto one of the dead branches and peered down at her. "Why stopping? Not goodly!"

"Dog ahead," Sly murmured. "Big dog."

Crow cawed his derision. "Dog being trapped behind metal web and chained to small house."

So they went on up the street. Little Fur's legs trembled because the horrible noises the dog was making were actually screams of rage, and *she could understand them.*

"I smell you!" the dog snarled. "Come close and I will tear and bite you. My fangs will crack your bones! I will pull you to pieces and eat you

up! I will eat the moon! I will crack it like an egg. I will slurp up the light in it and all will be darkness!"

"Do not be afraid," Sly commanded. "That dog is all bark and no bite. It wants to frighten us. That is what the humans trained it to do."

"The humans want it to frighten us?" Little Fur asked, but Sly sprang back to the web and began winding back and forth before it, crooning.

"I smell you, Cat," the dog growled, and Little Fur saw it loom as a huge, dark shape behind the web of metal. "I have killed a million cats," it whispered. "I have sucked them out of their fur. I will tear and bite you. My teeth will—"

Sly gave a long, chilling warble that made Little Fur's hair stand on end. "Cur. Slave and idiot who cannot hunt but must be fed dead meat by human hands."

Little Fur saw the dog clearly then. It was as tall as she was, with a chest broader than Brownie's and a coat so short it was like a skin clamped about the hot-smelling muscles of its body. Its head was wedge-shaped and massive, with a gaping maw that hung open to allow its red tongue to loll out between gleaming teeth. White-frothed drool hung from its bottom lip and there was a red shine in its eyes.

"Jump into my yard, Cat, and I will show you what I am," the dog invited.

Sly swayed close enough that the dog could have licked her face, had it not been for the fence. She showed no fear. Indeed, her smell was cruel and amused. "What could a tame beast like you do to a wild thing such as I? Tell me that, Pet?" she taunted.

This last word seemed to madden the dog. It threw itself violently against the web, which creaked and bulged out toward the cat but did not give way. Instead, there was a white flash of light and a loud clap as the dog was thrown yelping and howling into the dust of its yard.

Little Fur cried out once in fright at the flare of light, but the dog went on whimpering for some time. When at last it rose, it staggered as if it had been hit on the head. It came slowly right up to the fence, and Little Fur gagged, not at the singed smell it gave off, but at the rich, dreadful reek of its hatred. "I will know the scent of you again, Cat, and the scent of the thing from the last age that stands behind you. And next time, there will be no fence. . . ."

Sly gave a sniff and continued on down the lane, her tail high and haughty. Little Fur followed on shaking legs, as much appalled by the cat's deliberate cruelty as by the dog's hatred.

"What happened back there?" she asked to stop herself thinking of what might have happened if the dog had gotten through the web to them. "What made that light and the burning smell?"

"The web burned the dog!" Sly's eye flashed with sneering triumph. "Humans spin sky-fire into the metal web."

"I . . . I didn't realize they could do that."

"They can do anything they can imagine," Sly said carelessly. "The dog knows that the fence bites and burns but it is easy to make dogs forget because it is easy to make them angry. Things that are angry are always stupid."

"Why did you make it jump at you?" Little Fur asked. "You have made it your enemy by doing what you did. It won't forget you and it will try to hurt you if it smells your scent again."

Sly only gave her a cool look. "I am not afraid of a dog," she jeered.

But I am, Little Fur thought, for the dog had sworn to remember *her* scent as well.

They followed the metal web, and the cluster of huts behind it gave way to a vast, bleak plain scraped bare of all green and growing things. There was nothing on it except a few glimmering puddles that smelled like the road-beast feeding place. Little Fur was so aghast that she almost failed to notice that the cobbles had ended. The street had become one of the black roads and it stretched away into the distance. There was a track of stubbled grass between the black road and the web, but it was dangerously close to the web full of sky-fire.

"I don't think I can go along that," Little Fur said, remembering the terrible singed smell of the dog.

"Not following fence. Must crossing wasteland." Crow had landed by a gate in the web.

"What about the sky-fire?" Little Fur asked nervously.

"No sky-fire in gateway," Crow said, and to prove it, he flew to the top of the gate.

"What is this place?" Little Fur asked, staring through the fence at the bleak plain.

"Once here being grass and trees and empty stone dwellings. Good roosting for many birds. Then humans bringing roaring road beasts with long claws and great metal teeth to break everything to pieces. Maybe humans will building more high houses here. Or maybe this being new road-beast feeding place."

Little Fur had seen too much to disbelieve this. Crow must have smelled the sinking of her heart, for he added, "After this being grass plain. Then we coming to burying ground."

So Little Fur squeezed through the gate, but she had taken only a single step when she staggered back, pale and horrified. "The ground is dying!"

"Must crossing quickly then," Crow urged.

"You don't understand. It's dying because the earth spirit has just left it! You must find another way!"

Little Fur was pacing up and down the cobbles willing Crow to hurry when a thought struck her. She sat down and emptied the contents of the seed pouch onto her cloak. At the very bottom were several small seeds with dagger-tip points. They belonged to a greedy plant that would happily and swiftly strangle anything growing nearby. She gathered them only for their juice, which healed various forms of claw rot. But if she could bear to plant the voracious things in the ravished ground, they might just take hold swiftly and vigorously enough to summon the flow of earth magic.

She set pouch and bottle and cloak aside and went back along the street to get some moss. Then she squeezed back through the gate and pressed the moss onto the bare earth, knowing

that the good earth adhering to its roots would help shield the seeds so they might have a chance to germinate. Touching the moss protected her from the worst of the dying earth's pain, but she could easily tell that the ground had not only been savagely stripped of life, it had been deliberately poisoned.

That was what had driven the earth spirit away.

Little Fur got shakily to her feet and squeezed through the gate again. There was only a slim hope that the seeds would survive, but she had done her best. She went to the step of the stone dwelling where Ginger had curled up to sleep and sat by him, staring across the street at the ravaged earth. Then she lay against his soft flank and gave herself up to the soothing beat of his blood.

CHAPTER 12

The Wasteland

She woke to darkness and the scent of humans.

Ginger was already mantling himself in cat shadow when Little Fur peeped out of the doorway to see three humans standing at the open gate in the metal web. They were staring at the ground. A cold wind seemed to blow through Little Fur, for they were looking at the patches of moss where she had planted the seeds.

The biggest of the humans, a gross creature stinking of greed, pointed savagely at the moss. Its companions cringed, giving off the hot, acrid scent of their fear. Little Fur wished that she could slip away, but the humans were too close, and one of them carried a small square box spilling bright false light in all directions that swallowed the shadows which might have hidden her.

The smaller humans were speaking to the big one now, their voices full of pleading. Then, just as Brownie said sometimes happened when he listened to humans, a picture came from their words into Little Fur's mind of the two smaller humans spilling a milky liquid onto the ground and looking nervously about them every few steps. Little Fur understood immediately that it was they who had poisoned the wasteland. The bigger, dominant human had ordered them to do it and, seeing the moss, thought they had disobeyed.

Without any warning, the big human lashed out at one of the smaller ones, and it fell to the ground with a cry of pain. Little Fur thought the bigger human would kick it then. She smelled that it wanted to, but the one on the ground seemed to be holding something up. Then she saw what it was.

Her precious cloak!

The dominant human ground its heel into the moss, shaking the cloak as if it wanted to strangle it. Little Fur's hair stood on end at the thought of what it would do if it got ahold of her.

Ginger spoke urgently into her ear. *"Do not move."*

The big human was shouting orders and the other two took short metal tubes from their coats and held them out. Powerful beams of light slashed out into the darkness as they went through the gate. One went left and the other right, their beams of light cutting this way and that as they moved across the poisoned earth.

They are hunting for me, Little Fur thought, and trembled.

The big human remained by the gate, striding back and forth swinging the light box, stopping now and then to glare at Little Fur's cloak. Its heavy black eyebrows were drawn low over

its glittering eyes. Little Fur smelled that it was thinking hard, and that its mind was clever and subtle. She knew that it was only a matter of time before it thought of looking in the street, and a desperate desire to flee filled her.

"Wait," Ginger said. She smelled that he was moving away from her and feared that he meant

to attack the big human as he had the greep. But a few minutes later there was a cry from the wasteland. The big human turned and plunged through the gate, running after the others.

Little Fur knew that Ginger had given her one chance to escape. She crossed the cobbles, took a steadying breath, then stepped carefully onto the track of grass running alongside the fence. All of her senses strained backward to the humans on the other side of the fence, trying to discern where they were. But her fear and the closeness of the dying earth confused her senses.

The webbed fence suddenly changed direction, and Little Fur stopped. She would have followed it, because that was the way Crow had said they must go to reach the burying place, but there was too much of a risk that the humans would catch her with their stabbing lights. She struck out across a grassy slope that ran up and away from the bleak wasteland. Despite her fear, Little Fur thrilled at the strong, clean feel of the earth and air. Unfortunately, there was no tree or shrub or even a hollow where she could hide herself and her senses told her that the sun would soon open its eye.

At last she came to a ragged stand of bushes and stopped, feeling less as if the Troll King were slavering at her heels. She drank a brackish mouthful of the remaining water from her bottle, glad that she had slung it and her pouch over her head before going to sit with Ginger, or they would have been left behind as well. She would not let herself think about the dreadful loss of the cloak.

Instead, Little Fur set herself to listening and was reassured to hear nothing but the sighing of the wind. She decided to rest a little in the hope that Ginger would find her, but when more time had passed, she was forced to go on alone, lest she be trapped there when day came. She told herself that the cats could follow her trail and Crow would fly ahead since he knew the way to the burying place. The best thing to do, Little Fur decided, was to get there as quickly as possible. She didn't know exactly where it was, but she knew which way to go, and Crow had said it was not far.

Little Fur was almost at the top of the slope when she heard the roar of a road beast! She stopped, bewildered. Then a thick, painfully bright wedge of light bit into the darkness in front of her and swept this way and that. Instantly Little Fur understood that the big human had

found some way to get in front of her. She could not run back and she could not go forward, so she bent low and hurried sideways, praying that the slope would stop it from seeing her, for she could smell it now, the hot, urgent fury of its thoughts stretching out to her like claws.

As if the earth reshaped itself to help her, she had gone only a few steps before she fell headlong into a deep, lanelike ditch. She was astonished to find two lines of metal running along it, exactly like the rails she had followed before. But surely these could not be the same ones, even though they did go in both directions as far as she could see. Little Fur decided to follow them, because the ditch would hide her from the human if she crouched down.

She could not move very quickly while crouching, and she soon had a sore back and head from bending over so oddly. That might be what kept her from noticing that the ground had begun to rise. But when the ditch flattened out suddenly, she discovered that she had come up onto the beginning of some sort of structure which lifted the strip of earth beneath the metal rails high above true ground level. This must be what Brownie called a bridge, built by humans to let them go over things. Fortunately for her, grass and true good earth lay over the bridge, though she could not see what lay under it. A road, perhaps; maybe the very road the human had used to get from the wasteland to the top of the slope.

Little Fur started across the bridge. She had to move quickly because the sky was streaked with purple and orange now. The sun was very near to opening its bright eye, and the enormous human might yet be somewhere waiting for daylight to reveal her.

She had just reached the top of the bridge when a long, dreadful scream rent the air. It was so loud that it seemed to come from all directions at once, and there was a horrible metallic edge to it that hurt Little Fur and made her cry out and clap her hands over her ears. The scream seemed to go on forever and when it stopped,

the air quivered. Little Fur straightened and a sharp premonition of danger made her glance back. A monstrously long serpent of gleaming silver metal was writhing along the ground at an impossible speed, its single piercing eye casting a yellow glare before it.

So great was her wonderment that it was not until the metal rails began to vibrate and the earth began to shudder under her feet that Little Fur realized *it was coming along the rails*.

She turned and went on as fast as she dared, her heart thundering painfully in her breast. She reached true ground an instant before the great metal serpent came roaring and grinding over the bridge. She staggered away from the rails, but as the monster roared past, a wind pushed out like a giant hand and Little Fur fell forward. She managed to catch her balance, only to feel the earth give way under her feet. With a cry, she slipped and slithered down a smooth, hard slope into a swift, dark swirl of water.

CHAPTER 13

The Stone Fairie

Little Fur had fallen into a tumbling river. At first her shock was so great that she did not think to fight. It was as if she had fallen into a chilly dream. But then her heart began to bang and her breath to burn in her throat, and she thrashed her hands and kicked her feet until she reached the surface. She had time to gulp in a great breath of air, but then the current dragged her under again.

She floundered desperately against the force of the water, working her way toward the bank.

It was exhausting because if she rested an instant, she was at once pulled back to the center. The battle became harder the longer it went on, and as a deadly tiredness stole through her, Little Fur found herself wondering if it would be so bad to let herself go down into the liquid darkness.

A vision of the Old Ones, stately and green in their hidden hollow, came into her mind. A great longing to see them welled up in Little Fur, giving her the strength to go on fighting, but a moment came when she had no more strength left. She gave in to the flow, only to find that she had made it to the edge. Indeed, her feet were dragging on the ground and, fortunately, the bank nearest to her was curved enough so that the main force of the river passed by.

It took an immense effort of will for Little Fur to haul herself halfway up the bank. She was utterly spent. She did not faint or sleep, but for a time it seemed that her mind had been left behind in the dark, violent water, being smothered and swept along.

When she returned to her senses, the eye of
the sun was glaring down at her from overhead
and her legs were numb. Little Fur rolled onto
her back, dragging her feet clear of the river. The
bank sloped gently where she had come ashore,
but it mounded steeply upward before her,
hiding what lay beyond. She rubbed life back
into her legs and then reached for her water bottle, only to find that it was gone. Her pouch was
safe, though the seeds in it would need drying out
and some would be ruined. She groped anxiously
for the stone which she wore around her neck
on a plaited reed and was relieved to find that it,
at least, was safe. It was all that remained of her

mother, as the cloak had been all that remained of her father. Then she chided herself for thinking of *things* when she might so easily have lost her life.

It was not until she got up that it came to her that for the first time ever, her feet had left the earth, when she slid into the river. But she could feel the flow of earth magic still. Was it possible that it flowed through running water? After all, fish lived in water, and green reeds and water plants. It was a mystery that she would have pondered more deeply, except that she heard singing.

A powerful curiosity filled Little Fur as she clawed her way up the mound, but when she lifted her head above the edge, she saw a *human*. She shrank back and froze, until she realized that she couldn't smell a human.

Gathering her courage, she lifted her head again. The human was still standing exactly as it had been, and she saw what she should have seen at once! It was a shape formed out of stone, like the one she had seen in the beaked house.

There were other stone shapes around it. In fact, there were stone shapes as far as she could see in all directions, some human and some made into the shapes of animals. Still others were simple stone tablets.

She was so engrossed in them that she almost failed to notice a pack of real humans moving along a grass path toward her. She slipped quickly into the shadow between two square stones, half expecting to hear one of them cry out. She was so close that she could smell their grief.

The humans straggled to a halt and stood close together, their backs hunched against the wind. Little Fur could not see what they were doing but she could smell that the earth lay open in their midst. One of the humans began to speak and some of the others listening wept aloud. Little Fur could smell memories rising and swirling about the group.

Then, to her infinite wonder, *all of the humans began to sing.*

The sweetness and beauty of their song took her breath away, but more than that, she was astonished to smell that as they sang, their grief was gentled and lightened. It was as if their singing was healing them!

She crept away, moving from stone shape to stone shape, though she had the feeling the humans would not notice her even if they looked right at her. Their grief was like the current in the river, pulling them inside themselves. She had never smelled sorrow like that before. When she was far from the group of humans, she gazed up at the stone shapes, seeing how many of the human ones had been made to look kindly and compassionate. Was it possible the stones had been shaped this way to console humans suffering from the blackness of their grief?

She noticed two big trees growing amidst the stone shapes and was suddenly eager for the familiar touch of bark. Maybe there would be a bird or some small creature nesting in them, one that could tell her the way to the human burying place. Then she caught the mouthwatering fragrance of cloudberries. A bush grew in the shade between the two trees, and Little Fur threw herself down beside it and crammed her mouth full of the pale, juicy berries, quenching thirst and hunger at the same time. Then she lay back with a sigh of contentment.

A small, leathery brown face with pointed ears was gazing down at her. Moss-colored eyes widened as they met her startled gaze, and the face twisted with alarm and vanished.

"Hey! Come back and talk to me," Little Fur called softly, sitting up. She had seen enough of the small creature to recognize that it was a tree pixie. She laid her hand on the bark of the tree behind her, wanting it to reassure its pixie, but its leaves began to rustle.

There was a frightened yelp and the pixie's face reappeared. "How did you do thad?"

"Come down so we can talk properly," Little Fur invited.

"You mean come down so thad you can eat me, Troll," the pixie accused.

Little Fur stifled a laugh. "Can't you smell that I mean you no harm?"

The pixie glared at her. "I hab a code."

"I can come up and shake hands if you'd like."

"Don't you dare. My tree will drop a branch od your head ad squash you!"

This time Little Fur did laugh. The tree rustled again and the pixie stared at her in disbelief.

"My tree says you are going to save all trees frob the human tree burners. Is it true?"

Little Fur said nothing and after a moment, the pixie ran down the trunk like a spider, nose pointed earthward, long twiglike fingers clinging to the bark. "I am Garoldi," he said. "Cad I offer you something more to eat? I hab little nut cakes ad honeydew to drink."

"That would be very kind," Little Fur said politely.

The pixie scurried away, returning a moment later with a cloth bundle. As they ate, he asked her again if she really meant to stop the tree burners.

"I am going to try," Little Fur said softly, spreading out the contents of her pouch to dry. Seeing he wanted more, she told him of her journey to the beaked house. His eyes grew wide when she described her capture and rescue from the greep, yet when she told him of the metal serpent that had come after her, Garoldi laughed, saying it was only a vessel that carried humans from place to place. A train, he called it.

This seemed so fantastic that Little Fur could not believe it. She asked the pixie if he had ever heard of a place where humans buried other humans. He shook his head, but to her surprise he said that there was a large wood beyond the field of stone shapes. Perhaps that was where humans buried other humans. She couldn't see it now because it began where the ground dipped down, but he would show her.

Little Fur wondered if this could be the wood that the Sett Owl had described. She might have come to it from another direction. Garoldi insisted on packing a little picnic of cakes and cloudberries, and before they went he gave her a gourd bottle to replace the one she had lost. Little Fur refilled her pouch, then used a few herbs she had kept aside to make a tisane for Garoldi's cold. The shadows were growing long by the time they set off.

As they made their way through the stone shapes, Garoldi assured her that humans never came after dark.

Little Fur asked the pixie why humans came to the field of stone shapes at all.

"They plant their treasures here in big boxes," he answered knowledgeably. "They put them in the ground and cover them with earth. Then they weep."

This was as mysterious as everything to do with humans. "What about the stone shapes?"

He shrugged. "Perhaps they leave them to frighten other humans away. Come this way and you will see my favorite stone shape."

He led her from the grass to a wide, neat path of earth that would have made her nervous if Garoldi had not seemed so sure that no humans would come there now. It was not until they were almost under it that Little Fur saw the enormous stone fairie with huge wings folded behind it. As with all of the stone shapes, the smell of human on this one was ancient but unmistakable. Garoldi was gazing up at it in wistful awe. It took a moment for Little Fur to notice that the stone fairie held a stone baby in its arms. The baby

was human-sized, but the fairie had been made hundreds of times larger than a true fairie. Its face was beautiful and wise, but its eyes were sorrowful.

As they turned away, Little Fur wondered very much who had made the stone fairie and how they had known what a fairie looked like.

They came quite suddenly to a fence made from metal strands running between posts of old gray wood. Beyond, as Garoldi had described, a grassy incline ran down to a dense line of trees.

"Be careful, Little Fur," Garoldi said.

Little Fur nodded and ducked under the wire. She had almost reached the wood when an impulse made her look back. The sun had just closed its eye and the pixie was still standing on the other side of the barrier at the top of the slope, a tiny, solitary figure with the stone shapes of humans looming behind him, limned in scarlet.

CHAPTER 14

An Ancient Cut in the Earth

Pushing through trees, Little Fur imagined Crow waiting at the burying place, clacking his beak in frustration, and Sly and Ginger by the river that she had fallen into, puzzling about what had happened to her.

Then her heart quickened and she forgot about the others because through the trees, she could see a clearing and in the midst of it was a great, dark crack in the ground, exactly as the Sett Owl had described. It ran the whole length of the clearing, she saw as she emerged from the trees, and was narrow and sharp-edged, as if a giant had slashed the ground open with his knife. She wanted badly to look down into it, but its edges were cracked and eroded and she knew they would give way at once if she trod on them. It was impossible to imagine that she would be able to climb into the chasm when she could not even get close enough to look into it, but the Sett Owl had told her that was what she was supposed to do.

Little Fur sat down and ate a nut cake and drank some water from the gourd bottle Garoldi had given her, thinking hard. At last she set the food and bottle aside and lay down on her belly. Spreading her arms and legs wide, she wriggled carefully forward until she could look down. Moonlight lit up the top part of the chasm, where weeds and scruffy plants grew precariously on little juts and ledges. Little Fur's spirit fell, for they would certainly crumble if she tried to step on them, but the troll part of her saw deeper and found stone places where she would be able to gain a safe foothold. She tried to see below the moonlit part of the chasm, but there was a brownish murk blocking the way.

Little Fur closed her eyes and sniffed. The first layer of smells was familiar: damp earth and small plants with clutching roots and worms burrowing. She sniffed again, searching under all of those smells, and then she found it: the scent of something utterly strange.

She thought of what Crow had said about things that slept not liking to be awakened, and all the doubts born as she pushed through the trees flocked back into her mind and swelled. The Sett Owl had made a mistake in sending her. How could someone so small and unimportant possibly save all of the trees in the city? That was a task for a hero, like those in the stories

Brownie told. Why, if it had not been for Ginger, she would have probably been slain by the greep, or given to the trolls.

Despair was like the current in the river, pulling her under, clogging her eyes and nose and ears so that she could sense nothing else. Little Fur wondered if Sly and Ginger had been secretly laughing at her silliness in thinking that she could stop the tree burners, because of course humans were too strong and strange to be stopped from doing anything they wanted. The only way to survive was to hide from them.

But when she was near to drowning in despair, the earth magic under Little Fur's body surged. It was as if someone had thrown cold water into her face, for she saw at once that the things she had been feeling had been shaped by whatever lay in the chasm.

Something was trying to make her give up and go away.

Again doubts arose, clouding her mind and strangling her will, but Little Fur forced the tide of dreariness back by thinking of the trees whose minds she had touched on her journey through the city, and the millions that she had not touched. She was not alone because they were with her now; they were part of the flow of earth magic, as she was, the flow that the Troll King wanted to destroy.

No matter how many doubts and fears she had, she had promised to enter the chasm, Little Fur told herself fiercely. She had promised the Sett Owl that she would try to wake the power that slept here. She crawled to the very end of the chasm, where it became a narrow crack, seeing that the ground was more stable here. She

would not wait for the others, because waiting would give despair a chance to steal her courage. She must go at once, while she was full of determination.

Little Fur climbed into the crack and began to clamber down. The troll part of her seemed to know exactly where to find handholds and footholds that would support her, and she moved down the face of the chasm as swiftly and easily as flowing water. Doubts still floated into her mind, but the more she resisted them, the easier it was to resist.

Then her foot dipped into something cold and damp. Little Fur looked down to find that she had reached the oily brown murk. She moved and the murk stirred slowly like thick mud. Realizing that she would not be able to see out of the chasm once she went deeper, she looked up. The sky was a long skein of darkness caught in the thin lips of the crack, and because the moon was not visible, she saw only a scattering of stars. For a moment she saw a shape at the edge of the chasm that might have been a cat, but she shook her head, convinced that it was another trick being played upon her mind to delay her or stop her from going farther.

She descended into the gloom and the air was thick and hard to breathe, but her feet and hands were sure. She climbed until her arms and legs ached, and then it occurred to her that perhaps the chasm had no bottom and she would be climbing forever. Fear flickered in her mind. She tried to think about the things the Sett Owl had said but she could not seem to remember them clearly. The elf part of her felt lost, but the stubborn troll part of her nature refused to care what she felt. She had made up her mind to climb into the chasm and she would do that, even if she had forgotten why.

Then quite suddenly, she was at the bottom.

The floor of the chasm was pale and sandy and very cold. The air was cold, too, and so brown and thick that Little Fur could hardly see a step in any direction. The vagueness and sorrow she had felt while climbing were much stronger now, but she recognized them as yet another attack on her will and resisted by concentrating on walking.

She had been going for a good while without seeing a single thing when she almost stepped into a wide pool of water. Its surface was so still that it was as if she looked at herself rather than a reflection. Little Fur knelt and peered into it, for surely all the mysteries of life would be answered if only she could look deeply enough.

A ripple ran over the surface. Little Fur was astounded to see the Old Ones in their hidden hollow. How her heart ached at the sight of them, and how fair they were. She sat gazing at them, and maybe she would have sat like that forever if sharp teeth had not suddenly nipped her ear painfully. She swung around and sprawled sideways into the cold sand, her limbs so stiff that she could not lift a hand to save herself.

Sly peered into her face, green eye narrowed. "What is the matter with you?"

"I . . . I don't know." Little Fur felt confused

as she struggled to sit up. "I looked into the pool and I saw the Old Ones. Then you came."

"We saw you going down," Sly told her. "But that was hours and hours ago. We thought something must have happened to you, so I came to see."

"Hours . . ." Little Fur was stunned. Surely she had only just climbed down into the murk, and yet she was so stiff. Then it came to her. "Something has been trying to stop me coming down into the chasm and this pool must be part of it," she murmured. She resisted the urge to look again at the mesmerizing surface of the water as she got to her feet.

"Something is over there," Sly said.

They went on and found nothing but cold, pale sand and more brown mist. Then Little Fur noticed an enormous dead tree standing up against the wall of the chasm. A face had been carved deeply into its bark. Only a human would do such a thing, Little Fur thought; afterward the tree must have been pushed into the chasm, for the Sett Owl said that no human had ever come here.

She reached out, wondering if there would be anything of its dream left in the withered gray bark. She gasped, for the moment her palm touched it, she realized that it was not a tree but some gigantic treelike being. Nor was it dead.

Suddenly certain that it must be the very being she was supposed to wake, Little Fur closed her eyes and let her thought flow into the creature. It was not a tree, but it was very like a tree, and it was so deeply asleep that it was close to death.

Sly came gliding nearer, her broken tail twitching. "If you have a knife, you must cut it," she said. "Then it will wake."

"No!" Little Fur said, not liking the smell of cruelty in the black cat's words. She looked into the gnarled face of the creature and saw the faintest glimmer of greenish light under one drooping eyelid. She laid her hands against its bark again.

Then Little Fur began to sing.

She sang of spring mornings when the birds darted in the branches, shouting cheekily at one another; of the smell of dew-damp honeysuckle and new green grass. She sang of feasting on plump, fresh mushrooms in the shade of the trees, and of harvesting seeds in the golden days of Leaf Fall. She sang of winter and of trees and beasts falling into a deep sleep that would last until the warmth of the spring sun fell on them. She sang of the world waking finally after the long, deathlike sleep of winter, and at last she felt something in the creature stir. But it was like seeing a ripple on the surface of a lake and knowing a fish was far below. She must go on. She must crack that sleep open.

This time, she sang of the humans; of their

building of black roads and shining high houses; of their road beasts and of greeps and the poisoning of the earth.

The tree creature did not stir.

Desperate now, Little Fur sang of the tree burners and of their pact with the Troll King. She sang herself to silence, for not only did the creature fail to wake, it seemed to settle deeper into its sleep, so that death was but a whisper away now. Little Fur would have wept with disappointment, but she was so tired that she cast herself down at its roots and slept.

She dreamed vividly of the Old Ones, and of the tree burners climbing down into their hidden valley with fiery torches and savage curses. But then she dreamed of the earth magic surging through her. With it came a vision of the small human in the tree whose joy at seeing her had been so very sweet. She saw the old human at the beaked house who had smelled of kindness, and the humans on the field of stone shapes who had sung their bitter sorrow away. It was as if the earth spirit were telling her that the fate of the trees was bound up with the fate of humans.

Then she was dreaming of the Old Ones, and, in the dream, she began to sing her love to them.

CHAPTER 15
An Awakening

"Wake, Halfling," said a deep, thrumming voice.

Little Fur yelped in fright to see the enormous tree creature bending over her, its eyes as green and bright as emerald pools of water. "Your song of love woke me. It was very beautiful. Perhaps even beautiful enough to be worth waking to such a dark dream as this."

"This is not a dream," Little Fur whispered.

"Indeed it is. All life is a dream," the creature said ponderously. "Do you know what I am? Perhaps there are stories of me and my sisters that have leaked from other dreams into this one. Tree guardians, we are called."

Little Fur shook her head, hoping it would not be offended by her ignorance. "Maybe others came before who would have known. . . ."

"No one has come here before," it said. "Those who might have done so were repelled by the bleak dream which I brewed in the chasm. If that had not turned them away, the pool would have shown them their heart's desire, so that they would never look away from it."

"That's cruel," Little Fur couldn't help saying.

"Why? They would die with a vision of their dreams before them."

Little Fur was reminded of an elderly tree pixie who dwelt in the wilderness and was given to gloomy reflections whenever he made a rare appearance. Brownie said this meant the pixie was a philosopher and the only way to deal with philosophers was to be very clear and practical with them. Surely this creature, too, was a philosopher. So Little Fur got to her feet and smoothed

her tunic before saying firmly, "Excuse me, but I came to ask you for magic to stop humans from burning trees."

The tree guardian sighed. "Once, in another dream, I helped humans who yearned to nurture and harvest the wild world. That dream became a nightmare, for their true desire was to enslave all that was wild and use it for their own purposes. Now you tell me that humans are burning trees. It does not surprise me. But I have no magic that will stop them—no seeds to plant, from which warriors will grow to destroy them, nor rings that will let you bend their will to your own."

"I don't want to destroy them or bend anyone's will to mine," Little Fur said hastily and with some alarm.

"You don't? Then what do you want?"

Little Fur had not imagined that she would have to tell the sleeping power how to stop humans from burning trees, but the tree guardian was waiting and it seemed to her that it would wait for years. So she frowned and thought hard, and at last she gave a little cough.

"Yes?"

"Well, you could make humans understand."

"Understand?"

Little Fur saw that there were motes of gold moving slowly in the depths of the tree guardian's green eyes, like fish swimming in a deep pool. "You see," she said hesitantly, "I have learned in my journey here that not all humans are bad. I thought they were, and that they couldn't help it because they were made that way. I thought the badness was part of them like a bird's wing is part of it. But then I smelled humans that were not bad, so maybe badness is something that they could decide about—if they realized they could decide. So if you have the power the Sett Owl says . . ."

Her voice failed because the green eyes positively blazed at her. "I do have the power, Halfling. But when I and my sisters withdrew from the dark dream we had helped to build, we vowed to meddle no more in dreams, for do they not all fail in the end? I do not know where my sisters went, but I came here, and after ensuring that I would never be disturbed, I sank my will into a sleep so deep that the dream of life that grew here barely touched me . . . until your song woke me."

"I'm sorry I disturbed you, but the whole world isn't like this chasm," Little Fur said eagerly. "Why, the moon is—"

"The moon is no stranger to me, Halfling," the tree guardian said heavily. "I knew her when she was young. She, too, has seen the rise and fall of many dreams. I cannot help you."

Its voice was so stern and certain that Little Fur did not know what to say. She did not have the silver tongue of Brownie or the sober authority of the Sett Owl, or even the dramatic insistence of Crow. She saw that shadows began to shift in the tree guardian's dimming green eyes and realized that it was going back to sleep.

"Please," she cried. "Couldn't you try?"

The tree guardian said nothing, but a flare

of gold in the deep green eyes gave Little Fur the courage to go on. She clasped her fingers together as she took a step closer to the tree guardian, feeling suddenly that this was her last chance to save not only the trees and her beloved Old Ones, but the earth spirit itself.

"You see, if this world is a dream, then you are part of it. And dreams don't fail by themselves. Everyone who believes in them has to stop believing first." Little Fur swallowed. "And sometimes maybe you have to believe even when it seems hopeless. That's why I came to try to wake you when the owl said someone must. I thought a hero was needed, but now I think there are no such things as heroes except in Brownie's stories. There are only things that must be done and somebody must try to do them."

She did not dare to look into the tree guardian's eyes for fear of seeing that the shadows in them had gathered more thickly. But after a long pause, the tree guardian said, "Perhaps it is true that my sisters and I abandoned our dream. And so, I will send a dream to the humans."

Little Fur was dismayed, for she did not see how a dream could do very much to help. But the tree guardian smiled as if it saw her thoughts. "The dreams of my kind are not the greedy dreams of humans or trolls, nor the bright, high dreams of elves. They are powerful"—and now its eyes were kind—"though perhaps only a little more powerful than the dreams of halflings."

"What . . . what dream will you send?" Little Fur asked timidly.

"You have asked that I make humans understand and so I will unravel the dream they have made and let them see how their choices have shaped the world." The tree guardian heaved itself forward with a great shuddering and creaking onto thick, rootlike legs and lumbered awkwardly through the brown mist.

Little Fur followed, coughing at the dust it stirred up. When the tree guardian came to the edge of the pool, it stopped and raised its branch-like arms. Then it began to chant. The sound was musical and monotonous at the same time, changing tone sometimes to become softer or louder, but never faltering. The tree guardian stopped chanting for a moment and said, "Watch if you will, Halfling, but take care not to touch the water."

Then the chanting continued. Little Fur looked warily into the pool and was amazed to see one of the human high houses reflected. A cement path ran around it, bounded by a black road upon which a great, impatient herd of road beasts crowded, hooting and growling and huffing their impatience.

For an instant, the high house stood gleaming and perfect, but then humans appeared and began crawling over its surface, as industrious as ants. Where they went, black gaps appeared and spread, and the shining carapace gradually peeled back to reveal the complex innards of the building. The humans labored, carrying away bits of it until only its gleaming metal skeleton remained. Then this began to be cut away by great road monsters with long arms that had appeared beside the building.

Above the shrinking high house, the eyes of the moon and sun blinked rapidly from one to another until there was nothing at all left but a hole gouged in the ground and humans toiling to fill it. Black patches were beginning to show on the other high houses that had stood around it, and suddenly a big, low building appeared where the hole had been. Again, humans came to swarm over it and holes appeared, but it was not until trees began to spring up that Little Fur understood what she was seeing. *The pool was unmaking time.*

Soon all of the high houses were gone and the city was shrinking inward like a puddle of water drying up. All around it trees sprang into lovely, stately life. Black roads narrowed and melted away to become stony roads and then earthen tracks through dense woods; finally grass flowed over the worn tracks in a green tide. The sight was so lovely that it made Little Fur laugh aloud.

At last there was only a single cloth hut. A human emerged from it carrying an ax that glinted in the sunlight, and strode backward into the forest. It passed beneath all the wondrous majesty of the great trees without seeming to see them. Its expression was grim and brooding as it

stopped beside a fallen giant of a tree. It watched as the tree rose gracefully to join its stump. The human moved forward and hacked at it with the ax, but instead of the ax's cutting into it, pieces flew back into place until the tree was whole. Little Fur saw the human's expression shift from arrogance to fear and then to confusion and, last of all, to awe. Now its expression was fair and its eyes shone with wonder.

"What changed it?" she whispered.

"At first the heart of the human was touched by the beauty and age of the tree, but then it saw how short its own life was and it became afraid. The human hewed the tree to sever itself from the flow of life," the tree guardian said. "It wished to be only itself and to control all other things without having to care about anything but its own wants. But watch. It has not ended."

Little Fur looked back into the pool and gasped, seeing trees burning. The sight was all the more appalling after watching the forests restored to life. Through her tears, she saw the tree burners at their dreadful work, brandishing fire torches and laughing with mad, furious joy. Then she saw, very close and clear, the soot-smeared, fire-bright face of one tree burner after another. Then the vision faded.

"Now the dream is brewed, I will send it out to the humans and return to my sleep, Halfling," the tree guardian said.

"But . . . is that it? I mean, will the dream make humans choose not to be bad?"

"Halfling, those who sleep this night will dream my dream, and they will understand the darkness in their natures, but whether this will make them choose to resist it, I do not know. Maybe they will rub their eyes and forget the dream. Humans are very good at forgetting. Almost as good as they are at not seeing."

Little Fur was dismayed. "But the tree burners. Will they change?"

"They are wholly given to trollish visions, and their minds will not accept the dream. That is why I wove their faces into it. The other humans will know them now for their brutish deeds and prevent them from causing further harm."

"Will the other humans believe the dream?"

"Even if they do not, they will watch the tree burners closely and catch them when they act again."

"What is the darkness in humans?" Little Fur asked.

"They fear to die," the tree guardian said. "They think if they can control everything, then perhaps they will be able to choose not to die."

"But why?" Little Fur asked, astonished. "All things die and return to the earth. Death is part of the flow of life."

"Ah, but humans have cut themselves from the flow and so they see their dying as an end. That makes them want to destroy anything that will live longer than they do, or which reminds them that they will die. But now look, the dream goes into the world."

A thick green vapor was rising from the pool and coiling into the air to mingle with the murk.

Very slowly, brown gave way to green and the air went from being thick and dry to being as damp and sweetly scented as the wilderness after a spring shower. Little Fur sent her own longing into it just as she sent her mind inside trees, and she had the strange sensation of being unraveled into the mist.

Then it was over.

Little Fur felt that she ought to feel triumphant, but instead she felt strangely sad.

The tree guardian's eyes were kind. "You are weary, Halfling, for you sent your own song into the dream I brewed, and who knows what that will mean."

Little Fur struggled to open eyes that had closed without her quite knowing it had happened, but when she managed it, she could see neither the tree guardian nor the pool. All of the world had become a shifting green fog-cat, winding itself about her.

"Sleep, Halfling," the tree guardian whispered. "Dream your dearest desire, and I will dream it with you."

CHAPTER 16

Seeds

Little Fur dreamed that she was walking over hills and valleys of mist. Ginger paced at her side, and Crow flew overhead. Then all at once she was alone and hurrying down the rabbit track winding into the hollow where the Old Ones stood. When she was among them at last, her heart gave a great salmon-leap of gladness. The seven great trees had never looked more lovely to her than in that moment, all silver-sheened in the tender pink light of the sun's awakening, their leaves quivering in a breeze so faint that Little Fur could not feel it.

Then, to her everlasting delight, *the trees began to sing to her.*

Little Fur woke to the eye of the sun on her face and stirred at the unmistakable scent of fresh mushrooms.

"See, I *told* you it would wake her," Brownie said.

"Sun waking her," Crow snapped.

Little Fur smiled inwardly at their familiar squabbling and opened her eyes. She was lying in the broken leaf shade at the edge of the shadow cast by the Old Ones, and it was very early in the morning.

She sat up and Crow gave a startled scream.

"Are you all right?" Brownie demanded anxiously.

Little Fur touched his velvet muzzle softly. "Oh, Brownie, I am so glad to be back."

"But how we coming back? That is what Crow is wondering," Crow said.

Little Fur frowned. "Did I smell mushrooms?"

"Now I know you are all right," Brownie declared, neighing his laughter. "Eat, and then you must tell us what happened because I should go back to my field very soon."

Little Fur ate, wondering *how* to explain what she hardly understood herself. Had there really been a strange tree creature in the chasm that had brewed a green mist of dreams to stop the tree burners? Wasn't it just a story she had told herself? And how had she returned to the wilderness with Crow?

"Where are Ginger and Sly?" she asked.

"Ginger was here with you and Crow when I came, but not Sly," Brownie said. "Ginger went to look for her. But what happened? Did you find a great power in the chasm?"

"I . . . I think so, but it is hard to remember."

"What was the power?" Brownie asked eagerly. "Was it a great elf or a dragon?"

"It was . . . well, it looked like a tree, but it said it was a tree guardian and seemed to think I ought to know what that was. I asked it to help us and it sent a dream to all the humans who were sleeping, showing them who the tree burners were." Little Fur stopped because what had happened in the chasm seemed all at once too rare and strange to talk about.

"That's wonderful!" Brownie cried, and he pranced and reared, kicking up his hooves in delight. "My human said the other humans want very badly to catch the tree killers, but they could never figure out who they were. Now they will be able to catch them and stop them."

"Dream," Crow said disparagingly. "Will dream be enough to making humans punishing tree burners?"

"The tree guardian's dreams are not like our dreams, Crow," Little Fur said. "They are stronger. I think that's how we got here, you and Ginger and I. The tree guardian told me to dream my heart's desire and it would dream with me. So I dreamed of us all coming back here. I don't know why Sly didn't come. Maybe she didn't want to."

There was much to do that day after Brownie had gone, for there were many birds and small creatures waiting for Little Fur to heal them. One poor sparrow had a crushed wing and would never fly again, and there was a baby bat whose paw had been broken. Each creature that she tended had heard of her quest, so that Little Fur found herself delayed by having to answer countless questions. In the end it was Crow who took to telling their story, and Little Fur hid a smile as the tale became more and more fantastical and impossible with each retelling.

When the sun closed its eye at last and the line

of patients
ended, Little
Fur left on the pretext
of gathering herbs to replenish her stores. Crow
was telling a crowd of small animals how he had
battled a fierce mad dog who lived in a web, like
a spider. In truth, Little Fur wanted a moment
alone. It seemed to her that she had hardly had
a chance to take in the strangeness of what had
happened, and maybe a part of her would always
be wanting quiet moments to wonder at it.

She climbed up past the thicket and sat on
the hillside facing the human high houses,
thinking of what the Sett Owl had said about
the desire of the Troll King to destroy the earth
spirit. He would gnash his teeth in fury when he

understood that his human servants had been thwarted. But soon his fury would turn cold and deadly, and he would begin to think of other ways to use humans against the earth spirit.

The Sett Owl had said she was supposed to stop the Troll King, and all at once she understood why she did not feel as happy as Brownie: because her quest to save the earth spirit was not over. How could it ever be over while the Troll King lived? She had won an important battle, but a war was unfolding, and it seemed to Little Fur that the war would be played out in the world of humans. *They* were the battleground and the trolls would never stop trying to claim them.

So someone must work to claim them for the earth spirit. The dream of the tree guardian might have helped some of them to resist their darkness, and perhaps some of them had woken with a longing to be part of the flow of life again. But many of them would wake and forget.

Little Fur had vowed in the moments after waking that morning never to leave the wilderness again, but she realized now that this was a promise she could not keep. She must go out of the wilderness into the human city as often as she could and plant seeds wherever there was earth that could nourish them, for each seed that grew would summon the earth spirit until the flow was strong enough to encompass humans.

She was small, but sometimes small things could do what greater creatures could not.

Acknowledgments

I would like to thank Suzanne Wilson, who began editing *Little Fur* with me; Nan McNab, who stepped into the breach to finish it so beautifully; and Janet Raunjak, who was so sweetly there every step of the way.

I would also like to offer heartfelt thanks to the artists who helped this decided non-artist: my partner, Jan; my brother, Ken; Peter Cross; Ann James; and most of all, Jirí Tibor Novák, whose own art so inspires me, and who gave so generously of time, technical advice and even equipment. Without these real artists, I would never have managed to put Little Fur onto the page. I also want to thank Marina Messiha, who so beautifully art-directed this book.

Additionally, I want to thank all of the above and others — fellow writers, friends and, in the case of Tibby, children of friends — who so ably defended *Little Fur* from my anxieties and despair.

And, as ever, I must thank the cafés and their generous owners and staff, who put up with me sitting for hours over coffee, working. I wrote *Little Fur* in Cafe 145, The Sea Grape and The Bay Leaf, all in Apollo Bay, and in the Contemporary Art Museum café in Prague.

ABOUT THE AUTHOR

Isobelle Carmody began the first of her highly acclaimed Obernewtyn Chronicles while she was still in high school, and worked on it while completing a bachelor of arts and then a journalism cadetship. The series and her short stories have established her at the forefront of fantasy writing in Australia.

She has written many award-winning short stories and books for young people. *The Gathering* was a joint winner of the 1993 CBC Book of the Year Award and the 1994 Children's Peace Literature Award. *Billy Thunder and the Night Gate* (published as *Night Gate* in the United States) was short-listed for the Patricia Wrightson Prize for Children's Literature in the 2001 NSW Premier's Literary Awards.

Isobelle divides her time between her homes in Australia and the Czech Republic.

Don't miss Little Fur's next adventure!
Available now from Random House Books for Young Readers

Little Fur:

A FOX CALLED SORROW

"Listen to me, Fox. If you wish to die, then you must give yourself wholly to a deadly quest."

Little Fur is mystified by the fox called Sorrow, whose strong spirit keeps him alive despite his wishes. Who or what has caused the scars on his body, and the deeper scars on his soul?
On their dangerous quest to uncover the Troll King's evil plans, Little Fur will learn much about the fox, and about cruelty and treachery. Finally, the very existence of Little Fur, her friends and the great earth spirit itself may depend on Sorrow, the fox who wants to die.

CHAPTER 1
A Storm of Omens

It was autumn, and as sometimes happens in that season of heavy golden light and falling leaves, a powerful storm began to brew itself. It sucked up secrets and hidden purposes like leaves, flinging them into the air as omens.

Humans, blind and deaf to all but their own desires, could not easily read such signs. But as the storm gathered, children tossed in their beds and threw up an arm as if to ward off a blow. Hidden in the shadows, greeps, once humans whose strange, dreadful appetites had dimmed their minds and twisted their bodies, had a blurred awareness that something bad was coming. But they felt only an ugly pleasure at the thought that someone might suffer.

Wild creatures living within the city, and even some of the tame beasts dwelling with humans, sensed the warnings that churned in the air. But most of the animals responded with no more than a surge of instinct. Squirrels rushed to check their secret hoards, and rabbits examined the roofs of their burrows; ants rushed hither and thither; birds fortified their nests and turned their eggs anxiously.

A dog chained in a bare stone yard sensed the rage and hatred in the omens. Half insane from thirst and mistreatment, she began pulling ferociously at her bonds, ignoring the chafing of the collar fastened about her neck.

In the city zoo, a lion roared and would not be soothed no matter how much bloody meat its keeper gave it, and two panthers wove about each other in a tapestry of apprehension. In another enclosure, a frenzy of monkeys mimicked the violence they scented in the wind.

A half-starved fox limped toward the outskirts of the sprawling gray city over which the storm spread its black and ragged wings. He stopped to sniff at the wind and to read the warnings and signals. But his anguish was so great that if the world were to end he would not have minded. He limped on.

Those few creatures left over from a previous age could read the omens clearly, for they had been born when all honored the wind, knowing it for a great herald. But such omens required brooding upon to be properly understood.

A pixie who lived at the edge of the inland city over which the storm churned paused in the grooming of his beloved tree to stare at the clouds. He was troubled by the knowledge that by morning the russet glory of its leaves would be torn away. But the roots of the tree ran deep and there would be new leaves in the spring. He touched the leaves tenderly, turning his back on the clouds and their omens.

A boil of trolls at the mouth of a pipe leaking poisonous filth saw a lurid slash of light along the underside of the bruised-looking clouds and fell to hissing and cackling in delight.

Only one being sought to unravel the signs. Not a creature from a past age of the world, but a crippled, raggedy owl who dwelt in a church that the animals thought of as a beaked house. This was no ordinary church. Raised at the very cusp of the last age, it was a place where humans had brought hope for hundreds of years. So powerful was the accumulation of their longing that a still and potent magic had pooled there. The owl, who had retreated, wounded, to this church many years before, was saturated in it.

The storm rattled the shingles on the steeple and ancient beams began to strain and warp. The owl tilted her head and listened. She watched the stained-glass windows flash with daggers of

storm light. Gradually the Sett Owl understood. *The vital earth spirit, which seeks to unite all living things just as a mother strives for peace among her children, will soon face a terrible danger.* The owl was not surprised to discover that the Troll King lay behind the threat. But try as she might, she could not discover what form the threat would take.

The magic within the Sett Owl allowed her to commune with the earth spirit. The owl learned more of the darkness that loomed, but little of what might be done to prevent it. Yet the earth spirit offered the fragile and unimaginably sweet scent of hope, not only for the world, or for this city where trees once sang, but for the owl herself, too.

The Sett Owl was very old, even among her long-lived kind. She desired to pass from life and join the world's dream, but the still magic of the church would not permit it. The owl had to wait until one came who would take her place.

There was a loud crack of thunder. The earth

magic that flowed about the old church surged. The Sett Owl had a clear, bright vision of the elf troll Little Fur. Small as a three-year-old human, with pointed ears and brambling red hair, the gentle healer dwelt in a secret wilderness within the city that was hidden from human eyes by seven magical trees. Little Fur had once gone on a perilous quest to protect those ancient trees, whom she called the Old Ones.

At first the Sett Owl thought the vision meant that Little Fur must again sally forth. Then she realized that the elf troll was not the *answer* to the danger foretold by the storm, but the *reason* for the Troll King's plotting. The owl considered summoning the healer, but what could she say to her? It was not as if Little Fur had done anything wrong. Indeed, the opposite was true.

The Sett Owl did not question the earth spirit further because, where the elf troll was concerned, the earth spirit made no predictions. Perhaps it was because her parents had been a troll and an elf. But whatever the reason, Little Fur possessed a quality that was truly strange: she was *random*.

The Sett Owl gave a wheezy sigh and wished that these matters might have waited for her successor, but it was not to be. Well, the earth spirit had urged her to seek knowledge. If she could amass enough small pieces of information, perhaps she would get a clearer picture of what the Troll King planned.

Not far away, the storm front approached the hidden wilderness, but Little Fur did not notice the darkening sky, let alone the omens and signs driven before the storm. She was absorbed in trying to remove a grass seed from the badly infected paw of a raccoon. Two rabbits, a mouse, three birds and a hedgehog awaited her attention, and her stomach was rumbling with hunger, for she had eaten nothing since the morning.

Little Fur was concentrating so hard that she did not notice the rain beginning to fall, or its strange bitter taste. She had managed to work the grass seed out and was gently rubbing in salve to treat the infection when the drops of rain began to fall with a force that scattered her remaining patients. Little Fur scooped up the raccoon and retreated under the branches of the nearest tree. In the spring, the tree's thick foliage would have provided good cover, but it was autumn and its few remaining leaves were being harvested by the rising wind and slashing rain.

If alone, Little Fur would have hurried through the rain to the hill that rose behind her, pushed through the crown of brambles at the top and dashed down the steep winding track into the valley where the Old Ones grew. Beneath their dense, magical canopy, she would be safe from any storm. But the raccoon was too heavy to carry far and she could not leave her. Little Fur knew, as any true healer does, that mending the flesh is only half the task of healing a wound or sickness. Carrying the raccoon carefully, she picked her way between the trees, staying under cover as best she could until she reached a hollow tree. She climbed into its belly and began to croon a song to the raccoon's spirit.

Gazing out at the sky as she sang, Little Fur noticed black thunderheads rising like phantom mountains above the trees. Lightning lashed across the sky, illuminating the distant human

high houses. The shining towers showed no sign of bending before the storm; only things that were alive had the sense to bow before such a force. The high houses looked impervious, whereas all about her the trees bent and creaked and lashed their branches. Yet Little Fur knew it would be the city that suffered the greatest damage. Many of the small animals and birds that lived there would be hurt and would come to the wilderness seeking her healing skills.

There would be injuries within the wilderness as well. Nothing serious, Little Fur hoped, for she did not like to imagine that life and death might flutter under her hands; it was too great a responsibility. Such matters ought to be brought only before noble creatures like the Old Ones or the Sett Owl. An unease crept into her bones, but she dismissed it, telling herself she must rest and prepare for the days to come.

Little Fur's thoughts drifted back to the high houses. She wondered if some human was also staring out at the storm, and whether it was fearful or unafraid. Once Little Fur could not have imagined that creatures as malevolent and violent as humans could fear anything. But she learned through her first, perilous journey into the city—and the many forays she had made afterward to plant seeds—that humans were as different from one another as the creatures of any other species.

Humans *were* dangerous, though. To remind herself of that, Little Fur had only to think of the animals she had healed whose injuries had been caused by humans. But she now knew that rather than being essentially evil, humans harmed and destroyed from fear or confusion, or even by accident, as much as from a love of violence. She had smelled their cruelty and hatred and anger, but she also had caught the delicious scent of human curiosity and heard the astonishing beauty and power of human song. What she felt now about humans was a mixture of inquisitiveness and wariness.

Little Fur had decided that humans were the way they were because they did not feel the flow of the earth magic, which joined all living things. Every time she planted a new seed, it would summon the earth spirit; Little Fur thought that if she could just plant enough seeds, the earth spirit would flow so strongly through the city that humans could not help but feel it. Then they would cease to trollishly loathe and despoil nature.

Little Fur knew that in a way, she was trying to heal humankind. The ambition made her want to laugh. She was so small and the city so large. Yet each time she set out into the streets, she could feel that her plantings were making a difference. The earth magic *was* flowing more strongly there than when she had first stepped out of the wilderness.

Little Fur curled around the sleeping raccoon and drowsed. Occasionally she opened her eyes to see the curtain of rain sway aside, offering a glimpse of the high houses. Sometimes the gleaming surfaces reflected the jagged lightning, making it look as if they had cracked like sheets of ice.

It was not until near morning that Little Fur slept properly. Shreds of storm omens followed her into sleep. She dreamed she was crawling through cramped, dank tunnels under the earth. She could hear the shriek of wind and the low, urgent growl of thunder, but it came from below rather than above, as if a great storm churned at the heart of the world. Little Fur was trying to find her way to it so that she could plant a seed that would heal its hurt. Then she realized she had lost her seed pouch. . . .

Little Fur woke to a dazzle of light and the elated song of a thrush bubbling out into the new day.